THE LAST JUDGEMENT

"The latest (mis)adventure of art historian Jonathan Argyll delivers its plot twists at a rapid clip right up to the closing pages . . . Pears keeps his readers well occupied."
—Publishers Weekly

"A solidly enjoyable series." *—Library Journal*

"A sophisticated, adventurous, and gripping story that is sure to hold wide appeal." *—Booklist*

"Fans of antique dealer-sleuth 'Lovejoy' are bound to take a shine to Jonathan Argyll, an engagingly shambling English art dealer-investigator with exquisite tastes and a limited income. *The Last Judgement* is a joy for readers who enjoy a complex plot set to clever dialogue with the often-nefarious goings-on of the international art market as a backdrop." *—St. Petersburg Times*

"Jonathan Argyll is clever and entertaining . . . Pears knows what he is talking about and tells a rollicking good yarn." *—Boston Globe*

GIOTTO'S HAND

"Fine art, quirky characters and scenes set in Rome and an English country village add to the joys of *Giotto's Hand* . . . A neat twist at the end is the cherry on this fudge sundae of a mystery." *—Minneapolis Star Tribune*

DEATH AND RESTORATION

MORE MYSTERIES FROM THE
BERKLEY PUBLISHING GROUP ...

THE HERON CARVIC MISS SEETON MYSTERIES: Retired art teacher Miss Seeton steps in where Scotland Yard stumbles. "A most beguiling protagonist!"
—*New York Times*

by Heron Carvic
MISS SEETON SINGS
MISS SEETON DRAWS THE LINE
WITCH MISS SEETON
PICTURE MISS SEETON
ODDS ON MISS SEETON

by Hampton Charles
ADVANTAGE MISS SEETON
MISS SEETON AT THE HELM
MISS SEETON, BY APPOINTMENT

by Hamilton Crane
HANDS UP, MISS SEETON
MISS SEETON CRACKS THE CASE
MISS SEETON PAINTS THE TOWN
MISS SEETON BY MOONLIGHT
MISS SEETON ROCKS THE CRADLE
MISS SEETON GOES TO BAT
MISS SEETON PLANTS SUSPICION
STARRING MISS SEETON
MISS SEETON UNDERCOVER
MISS SEETON RULES
SOLD TO MISS SEETON
SWEET MISS SEETON
BONJOUR, MISS SEETON

KATE SHUGAK MYSTERIES: A former D.A. solves crimes in the far Alaska north ...

by Dana Stabenow
A COLD DAY FOR MURDER
DEAD IN THE WATER
A FATAL THAW
BREAKUP

A COLD-BLOODED BUSINESS
PLAY WITH FIRE
BLOOD WILL TELL
KILLING GROUNDS

INSPECTOR BANKS MYSTERIES: Award-winning British detective fiction at its finest ... "Robinson's novels are habit-forming!"
—*West Coast Review of Books*

by Peter Robinson
THE HANGING VALLEY
WEDNESDAY'S CHILD
INNOCENT GRAVES

PAST REASON HATED
FINAL ACCOUNT
GALLOWS VIEW

CASS JAMESON MYSTERIES: Lawyer Cass Jameson seeks justice in the criminal courts of New York City in this highly acclaimed series ... "A witty, gritty heroine."
—*New York Post*

by Carolyn Wheat
FRESH KILLS
MEAN STREAK
TROUBLED WATERS

DEAD MAN'S THOUGHTS
WHERE NOBODY DIES
SWORN TO DEFEND

JACK McMORROW MYSTERIES: The highly acclaimed series set in a Maine mill town and starring a newspaperman with a knack for crime solving ... "Gerry Boyle is the genuine article."
—*Robert B. Parker*

by Gerry Boyle
DEADLINE
LIFELINE
BORDERLINE

BLOODLINE
POTSHOT

THE
TITIAN COMMITTEE

Iain Pears

BERKLEY PRIME CRIME, NEW YORK

THE TITIAN COMMITTEE

A Berkley Prime Crime Book / published by arrangement with
the author

PRINTING HISTORY
Harcourt Brace Jovanovich hardcover edition / 1991
Berkley Prime Crime mass-market edition / May 1999

All rights reserved.
Copyright © 1991 by Iain Pears.
This book may not be reproduced in whole or in part,
by mimeograph or any other means, without permission.
For information address: The Berkley Publishing Group,
a division of Penguin Putnam Inc.,
375 Hudson Street, New York, New York 10014.

The Penguin Putnam Inc. World Wide Web site address is
http://www.penguinputnam.com

ISBN: 0-425-16895-6

Berkley Prime Crime Books are published
by The Berkley Publishing Group,
a division of Penguin Putnam Inc.,
375 Hudson Street, New York, New York 10014.
The name BERKLEY PRIME CRIME and the BERKLEY PRIME CRIME
design are trademarks belonging to Penguin Putnam Inc.

PRINTED IN THE UNITED STATES OF AMERICA

10 9 8 7 6 5 4 3 2

To Dick

THE
TITIAN COMMITTEE

CHAPTER

1

The initial discovery was made by the gardener of the Giardinetti Reali, an old and stooped figure whose labours generally pass unnoticed by the millions of tourists who come to Venice every year, even by those who eat their sandwiches amidst his creation as they get their breath back from overdosing on architectural splendour.

For all that he was underappreciated, the old man was obsessed with his job. In this he was rare. Venice is not noted for its enthusiasm for nature; indeed, its entire history has been dominated by the need to keep the elements from interfering in its business. A flowerpot hanging out of a window is generally the closest the inhabitants come to the joys of the wild. Most cannot even see an open space without imagining it neatly covered with stone flaggings. If you want to grow things, go to the mainland; real Venetians don't dig holes.

So the gardener felt himself to belong to a small and somewhat persecuted minority. A couple of acres of garden wedged between the Piazza San Marco and the Grand Canal. Flowerbeds to dig, grass to cut, trees to

prune and tend, sea water to keep at bay. All with little
help and less money. But today, Saturday, was a big day.
The City had especially asked him to provide flowers for
a banquet to be held on the Isola San Giorgio that evening. He would give them his best, three dozen lilies he
had been cultivating for months in one of his little greenhouses. They would be admired, and he would be
praised. A great day.

There was a lot to be done. Cut the flowers, trim them,
prepare them, wrap each one carefully and individually,
then send them off to take their part in the wonderful
arrangements which, he was sure, would be the talk of
the evening. So he got up early, just after six, downed a
coffee and a glass of *acqua vita* to get the blood going,
and set off in the chilly, damp weather of late autumn to
start work. Although cold and still not fully awake, he
felt a small surge of anticipatory pleasure as he neared
the greenhouse, looming up out of the early morning sea
mist that invariably hangs over the lagoon at this time of
day and at this time of year.

Until, that is, he opened the door and saw the crushed,
mangled and twisted remains of the upright and beautiful
flowers that he had so carefully tended. The exquisite
creatures he had left the night before were no more. He
could not believe his eyes. And then he saw the curled
up form of the drunken, late-night reveller in the middle
of the flowerbed who was evidently responsible.

He tried to restrain himself, but could not, and let out
his venom by trying to wake up the wretch with a well-
aimed kick. A woman. When he was young, women
knew how to behave properly, he thought bitterly. Nowadays . . .

"Damn you, move. Wake up. Look what you've
done," he shouted angrily.

No reply. He put the toe of his shoe underneath the unconscious figure and turned it over, so he could insult the destructive, malicious creature more effectively.

"Mother of God," he said instead. And ran for help.

"Murder," said General Taddeo Bottando, with a ghoulish smile on his face as he sat in his sunlit office in central Rome. "Murder," he repeated, evidently enjoying the word and the reaction that showed up on the face of the assistant sitting opposite him. "Bloody and violent," he added, folding his arms over his protuberant stomach, just to make sure there was no mistake in the matter.

It was Sunday, the day after the Venetian gardener had discovered the devastation in his flowerbeds. Since he had run, shocked and alarmed, to find a telephone and call the police, Italian officialdom had been thrown, if not quite into a frenzy of activity, at least into a state of decorous movement. As a result, General Bottando had reluctantly come into his office on his day of rest, and had summoned his assistant from her bed to help.

It is, after all, very thoughtless of anyone to go and die in a foreign land. Indeed, if travellers realised how much trouble it caused, most would undoubtedly delay their departure from this world until they got back home. Firstly, the local police have to be informed, and doctors, ambulances, pathologists and so on brought in to deal with the corpse. Then a message has to be passed to the consulate, which contacts the embassy, which contacts the authorities back home, who contact the local police, who have to inform next of kin. And that is only the start. When you add on the business of writing assorted reports in any number of languages, and organising the transportation of the body with the customs and immigration authorities, it is little wonder many officials wish that foreigners, if they must die, would do so elsewhere.

It is even more tiresome when the foreigner gets himself—or herself, as in this case—murdered. And when that foreigner is a member of an art historical committee funded by the Italian Arts Ministry—and the subject of the committee's work is Tiziano Vecelli (1486–1576), a Venetian, at a time when the Interior Minister is also a Venetian—telephones ring, telexes are sent, demands are made, bucks are passed. Everybody wants instant action, taken by someone else.

And hence, to return to the point, General Taddeo Bottando's complacent smile as he mentioned the circumstances of Professor Louise M. Masterson's untimely end to Flavia di Stefano, his best, brightest assistant in the Italian National Art Theft Squad.

"Oh good," replied his assistant, with relief. "You had me worried for a moment. So why am I here and not in bed reading the paper?"

It should not be thought for a moment that either of them was cruel or unfeeling in this matter. Had they thought about it, they would have been properly upset that a 58-year-old woman, in her prime and with much to offer in her chosen field of Renaissance iconography, had been prematurely sent to the grave by an unknown assailant. But it is one of the constants of police work that there is rarely enough leisure to think too much about matters that are none of your business.

And this death, tragic though it might have been, fell very clearly and obviously into that category. Their little department, small and underfunded, had been set up several years back to battle valiantly but hopelessly against the tide of thefts sweeping Italy's works of art out of the country. Its members dealt with theft and fraud concerning pictures, prints, drawings, statues, ceramics and even, on one occasion, an entire building that was stolen *en bloc* for transportation to South Korea. They were proud of having recovered one staircase, a room and part of the library. Alas, the walls and foundations were never seen again. It was, as Bottando explained to the distressed owner as he stared at the heap of rubble and woodwork in the back of the lorry, only a partial success.

The point was, that while crimes against art were in their purview, crimes against art historians were not. Such deeds were liable to be taken out of their hands, even if the entire contents of the National Museum had disappeared at the same time. Quite a lot, admittedly, depended on bureaucratic wrangling between the various parts of the assorted police forces, but a past master like Bottando would have had no trouble avoiding a case involving a murder if he didn't want it.

And surely he didn't, Flavia thought, trying to work out why she was not still in bed. It does you no good, no good at all, in the Italian polizia, to rush around volunteering for things. People stop taking you seriously. The thing to do is wait to be asked by some senior figure like a minister, then screw up your eyes in anguish, worry about how many other things you (or your department) have on your plate at the moment, then reluctantly agree that, as no one else is capable of dealing with such an urgent matter, your specialised skills might be made available. Solely because you hold the minister in such high personal esteem and, while on the subject, perhaps the minister might see his way to helping you with . . .

Something like this had been going on, Flavia was sure. The only question remaining to be resolved was what it had to do with her. She had a sneaking idea. The Italian state habitually overspends, running vast budget

deficits that have everybody outside the government running around and wringing their hands in despair. Peri-
odically, a new administration decides to tackle the
problem. Such efforts never last very long, but for six
months or so programmes are axed, departments cut back
and savings made. Then everybody gets tired of it, matters return to normal and the deficit resumes its usual
upward spiral.

The trouble was that they were in one of their periodic
bursts of austerity and the rival police force was floating
a money-saving idea to break up Bottando's department
by setting up members of the carabinieri in local forces
to deal with artistic thefts. It would be less effective and,
in the end, save no money at all, but Bottando knew well
that that was not really the point. The carabinieri had
never really accepted that his department had been set up
under polizia control. Normally he would have no trouble
in seeing them off, but at the moment he was a worried
man. His enemies were winning a hearing. The annual
budget submissions were due in eight days, and the
show-down was perilously close.

"Has this, perchance, got something to do with the
budgets?" Flavia asked, and groaned as he nodded.

"Oh, no. Please. Not me. I've so much work to do
already," she said desperately, looking at him with all
the mournful appeal her large, blue, north Italian eyes
could summon at such short notice.

But he was a hard man. "I'm sorry, my dear. I'm sure
we can redistribute your load."

"You couldn't when I asked you for a day off on
Friday."

Bottando was not, however, a man to be put off by
little details. "That was Friday," he pointed out with
accuracy, waving the matter aside with a chubby hand.

"Have you ever heard of the Titian committee?"

Flavia had worked with him long enough to know defeat when it stared her in the face. "Of course. Some vast, government funded enterprise to produce a complete catalogue of everything Titian ever did, down to authenticating his laundry bills? Quite a status project, isn't it?"

"Something like that," her boss replied. "The Dutch set up something similar, and the arts minister decided that if anyone was to have the prestige of a hugely over-funded international mega-project it should be an Italian painter, not some Dutch hack like Rembrandt. So they set up an even more pricey affair for Titian. Half a dozen experts, soaking up enough money in a year to keep us in luxury for a decade. A team effort. Don't know why but evidently in this bureaucratic age they think that six personal opinions are better than one. Makes it seem more accurate. Not so sure I'm convinced. They work away like fury, producing catalogues of paintings, drawings and so on. You know the sort of thing."

"I've heard of it," she said. "So?"

Bottando regarded her a bit doubtfully. "So," he said, labouring the word to show he'd noticed her lack of enthusiasm, "so, now there's only five of them. To put it another way, a sixth of this high-powered, international committee has gone and got murdered, that's so. And it's causing a bit of a stir in certain circles. That is to say, for various reasons the Arts Ministry, the Foreign Ministry, the Tourism Ministry and the Interior Ministry are all up in arms about it. And that's not counting the local authorities in the Veneto and in Venice itself. Fuss, fuss, fuss."

"I understand that. But it's a job for the local carabinieri, isn't it? After all, they must be used to it by now.

Foreigners die in Venice all the time. People write books on it.''

"Indeed. But it's not all that often that they're murdered. Anyway, the point is, it has been decided that the forces of Italian law and order have to do their best to sort this out. Experts flying in, national effort, and so on. And you, my dear, are the instrument chosen to demonstrate how seriously the government is taking this challenge to Venice's ability to draw in tourist income.''

"Me?" said Flavia with mixed astonishment and annoyance. "Why on earth send me? I'm not even in the police.'' Which was true, although she only remembered this fact when it was convenient. Technically she was only a researcher and had strenuously resisted the temptation to sign up on a more regular basis. Uniforms didn't suit her. Nor, for that matter, did the odd spurt of military discipline the polizia occasionally indulged in to remind its forces they were technically members of the army.

"Exactly," Bottando replied happily, pleased that she was so quick on the uptake at such an early hour. "It's all appearances, you see. Politics, in a word. The powers that be down here want to show they're trying. But they don't want to put the noses of the locals out of joint. So we are going to send, firstly, someone from the art squad to help out with our expertise and, secondly, someone junior who will not make the Venice carabinieri think they're being criticised. And that all adds up to you.''

"Thanks for the show of confidence," said Flavia with some pique. Which was a little irrational of her. She'd come into Bottando's office hoping she wasn't going to be given an investigation, and now found herself offended that she hadn't. It was, nonetheless, galling to think her main qualification for the job was being entirely innocuous. "I still think it's a complete waste of my time."

Bottando shrugged. "That depends on whether you want a job next month," he said reasonably.

A good argument. "Oh, all right. If I must."

"You mustn't think of it like that," Bottando told her reassuringly. "It's a wonderful opportunity. You have to do nothing at all, and will gain the thanks of three of the most powerful ministers in the government for not doing it. As will the department, of course, which is more important at the moment. Could be crucial in fact, if we get the timing right. Consider it as more of a paid holiday. You can trot up tomorrow, spend a day and be back home by Tuesday evening. Besides, Venice, I remember, is particularly beautiful at this time of year."

"That's not the point," she protested. Really, the man's willingness to ignore facts to suit himself was extraordinary. He knew very well she'd been planning to go to Sicily. Venice, however adorable, was not at all what she had in mind. But he paid no attention.

"You will have to put in an appearance with the police up there, but you can make it clear that you have no intention of interfering at all with their investigation," he went on, becoming all businesslike now he knew he'd won. He normally did, but Flavia was sometimes wayward over the matter of obeying orders.

"All you have to do is hang around, work on your expense account, then knock out a perfectly harmless report in which you sound brilliant and penetrating but exonerate everyone for not arresting the murderer while also making it clear that you have established that it is not a matter for our department. Standard sort of thing. That should do the trick nicely."

She sighed more openly so he would realise the sacrifice she was making for the public good. A nice man, an amiable soul, but a bit of a bulldozer in many ways. She knew him well enough to know a fight was pointless. She was going to Venice, and that was settled.

"You think they won't find whoever it was?"

"Shouldn't think so for a moment. I'm a bit hazy on the details but first reports make it sound like a mugging that got out of hand. I've no doubt you'll find out when you get there."

CHAPTER

2

By the time the internal Alitalia flight began its circling descent to Venice's Marco Polo airport bright and early on Monday morning, Flavia had forced herself back into a moderately good humour, despite having risen from her bed at an ungodly hour, yet again, to catch the plane.

Were it not for the circumstances, she would ordinarily have been overjoyed at the prospect of getting out of her under-ventilated, over-inhabited office in central Rome. Venice, after all, was not *such* a bad place to spend a day or two. As it was going to be a brief trip, she travelled as light as was compatible with being prepared for all eventualities. Trousers, dresses, skirts, shirts, sweaters, a dozen or so books. Maps of Venice and the surrounding area, railway and airport timetables, overcoat for the cold, raincoat for the rain. Boots for walking, good shoes just in case, pads of paper and notebooks, a few files of police business, towels, dressing-gown, gloves, a torch for emergencies. She would, probably, wear nothing except jeans and sweaters, as usual, but there was no harm in being prepared.

As the plane swept in, she occupied herself with tidying her hair and setting her clothes to rights. She wanted to look good as she got off at the airport. Such vanities she normally dispensed with; she was fortunate that she could afford to do so without it making much difference. Besides, no matter how much she combed, her hair would be a mess once the wind that always blew around Marco Polo had finished with it. But Venice is a place that demands that you make yourself presentable. It is an old and dignified city and insists on respect from visitors; even tourists occasionally try to make themselves look less unsightly than usual once they fall under its spell.

She started as she meant to go on. Bottando had insisted it was important she spend as much money as possible, and she intended to follow his instructions. The value of her presence would be calculated in direct proportion to the size of her expense account, he had said, not by what she got done. This, among the more cynical of her colleagues in the department, was known as the Bottando Ratio. If the government was to convince itself that the department had played a crucial role in trying to resolve this unfortunate affair, then the bill would have to be a hefty one.

So she shunned the public water bus into the city and settled herself into the back of one-of the long, varnished motor taxis that ply their trade between the airport and the main island. No airport in the world has a more beautiful approach to the city it serves. Instead of a bus crawling along crowded motorways or a train through industrialised desolation, you rush through the lagoon, past crumbling islands until Venice itself peeps up over the horizon. Apart from the fact that the ride made her feel a little queasy, it was a glorious experience, especially in weather which was perfect, despite the presence of some not very encouraging clouds.

The driver, suitably sea-worthy in black T-shirt, cap and red neck-scarf, piloted with skill and speed along a route marked out by ancient lumps of wood sticking up above the surface of the glistening water. He paid her little attention, beyond the obligatory wink and flashing smile as he helped her in and stowed her luggage. The other occupant was much more inclined to pass the time of day. Had Fellini ever decided to film "The Rime of the Ancient Mariner," this was the man for the title role. His face was a piece of old driftwood, and his age, if uncertain, was definitely over seventy. He was short, grizzled beyond imagining, had an appallingly-fitted set of dentures which clicked alarmingly when he smiled, and still seemed as though he could tear blocks of concrete in two with his bare hands.

He settled himself down beside her in the stern, beamed and clicked at her for several minutes, then embarked on his morning entertainment. Was she on holiday? Staying long? Meeting someone?—this with a sly glance—Visited Venice before? She answered patiently. Old men like to talk, like the company of the young, and besides, his curiosity was so intense that it could not possibly be objectionable. He was, he told her proudly, the father of the driver and had himself been a gondolier in Venice all his life. Now he was too old to work but liked occasionally to accompany his son.

"I bet you didn't have boats like this when you were his age," Flavia said, more to vary her conversational diet from a stream of yesses and noes.

"This?" the old man said, wrinkling up his face so that his nose almost disappeared beneath the surface. "This? Call this a boat? Pah!"

"It seems very nice," she observed vaguely, aware that this wasn't exactly the most nautical way of phrasing it.

"All flash and noise," he said. "About as well made as an orange box. They can't make boats any more. Can't do anything properly in the lagoon any more."

Flavia looked over the flickering, shining water to the island of Burano on her left, saw the seagulls whirling overhead in the wind and spotted an oil tanker peacefully chugging its way out to sea in the distance. The boat cut a creamy wave through the dark green water of the lagoon as it headed towards the city. "It all appears in proper order to me," she said.

"Appears, yes. But it's not appearances that count. They've forgotten about the flow."

"Beg your pardon?"

"Flow, young lady, flow. This lagoon is full of channels. Very complex, each one serves nature's purpose. They used not to disturb that. Now they chop huge paths through the lagoon to let things like that in." He gestured dismissively at the tanker.

"With the wind and the tide in the right direction, everything goes haywire. Just like that. Can happen in minutes. Water flows in the wrong direction, washes everything to the surface, floods and leaves it. Smells disgusting. Comes of trying to be too clever. The city's choking in its own muck because of their stupidity."

He was getting into his stride about the iniquities of the modern age when his son, glancing over his shoulder and evidently fearing for his tip, ambled back. Flavia wished he had stayed where he was. It was no doubt perfectly safe to leave an unguided boat hurtling through the water at high speed, but she would have felt more confident had someone been there just to make sure. A demonic driver on the roads, she was nervously cautious when it came to water. The result, no doubt, of growing up in the foothills of the Alps.

A few sharp words and the old man was dispatched forward to wrap some ropes, or whatever you do on boats, and she was left alone to study the scenery. Flavia watched with delight as the first signs of Venice itself rose above the horizon. The campanile, then the tower of San Giorgio, the crumbling brick of the Frari. More boats, buses, gondolas and the heavy working barges that ferried goods from place to place, appeared on the water. Then the crumbling brick and peeling stucco of the buildings on the main island itself, as the taxi swung around its northern end and headed for the Piazza San Marco.

The driver propelled his boat along at what seemed like an impossibly reckless speed, weaving in and out of the traffic, and aimed it at the side of the canal. He slammed the engine into reverse at the last moment, swung round and then, with a little flourish, brought it to a dainty, perfect halt at exactly the right place. The result of years of practice. Flavia paid, handed over a healthy tip and walked up the steps onto Riva Schiavoni, with the driver bringing up the rear with her bags.

Checking in at the Danieli Hotel took only a few moments. Again, she was obeying Bottando's instructions to the letter. It was not often she was virtually ordered to stay in the most famous and expensive hotel in the north-east of Italy, and she was determined not to let the opportunity slip. Ordinarily, the Danieli was crammed with the richer sort of German and American tourists, and even the monumental gothic lobby sometimes bore a striking resemblance to a bus station, with crowds of frantic tourists milling around afraid of being left behind and piles of luggage stacked in corners. But the season

was ending and, while tourists were still very much in
evidence, they had been culled to more manageable proportions. The staff were consequently less harried than
usual and, for Venetians, almost polite.

The room was delightful, the weather still sunny and
the bed remarkably comfortable. The only other thing
anyone might reasonably ask for was food, and she resolved to take care of that immediately. The trip in had
taken a good hour and it was well into Flavia's lunch
break, so she changed into more suitably professional-
looking clothes and headed back down the stairs. If Bottando had taught her one thing, it was that really good
and reliable policework could not be done on an empty
stomach. At the desk in the lobby she asked for directions
to the central questura, bought a newspaper in the shop
so she could see how the local press were reporting the
murder, and headed off for a hefty, if solitary, meal.

She was content and only slightly indigested as she
walked slowly up the steps of the questura at around
three that afternoon. The building was a very Venetian
affair. Evidently it had once been the palace of a noble-
man of substantial wealth, but it fell so far from its original glory that it was co-opted by the state and colonised.
Rooms that were once enormous and well-proportioned
had been divided, then subdivided, into dingy little cu-
bicles connected by even darker, more unkempt and depressing corridors. Whatever the budget of the local
police, very little of it went on keeping their headquarters
well decorated. All very economical and proper, no
doubt, but a pity. Her own department in Rome occupied
much smaller premises, but Bottando's ability to delay
handing back stolen works of art that were recovered (he
always quoted paperwork in order to hang on for a few

months to pieces he particularly liked) meant it was much more appealing to the eye. Very important for department morale, even if the best works tended to be stored for security reasons in his own office.

Her holiday mood was evaporating rapidly by the time she had wandered up and down for ten minutes hunting for her destination. It waned still further when she was shown into the office of Commissario Alessandro Bovolo and saw the small, ill-humoured man behind the desk, ostentatiously reading papers and pretending not to have noticed her arrival. But she had decided in advance to be the perfect colleague and was determined to give the man a chance. So she waited patiently, composing her face into cheery nonchalance. Silence fell, apart from the odd snuffle from Bovolo, the rustle of paper and the faint, but quite amazingly irritating, sound of Flavia humming quietly to herself. Eventually, Bovolo could stand her limited musical talents no more. He dropped the sheaf of seemingly absorbing documentation, smoothed down his lank, mousy hair and looked up with the air of an important man reluctant to be distracted.

By no stretch of the imagination could he be considered handsome, even in the best of circumstances. Late forties, he had a thin face, slightly pointy nose, blotchy skin and small colourless eyes. Apart from that, there was not much to be said for him. If one of the fishermen in the lagoon accidentally dredged up a large herring, dressed it in a crumpled grey suit and arranged it in a chair with a pair of wire-rimmed spectacles over its nose, the resemblance would have been extraordinary.

"Signorina di Stefano," he said eventually, with too much emphasis on the "signorina" for Flavia's taste. "The elegantly-dressed young expert from Rome come to show us how to catch murderers." The slightly watery smile that accompanied this made her suspect he was not wildly enthused about making her acquaintance. She was quick that way.

"From Rome, yes. Expert, no," she replied, deploying her sweetest and most disarming smile for the occasion. "Whatever the accomplishments of my department, catching murderers is scarcely one of them."

"So why are you here?"

"Solely to help if you decide you want it. We do know a lot about the art world, after all. General Bottando was very much of the opinion that my assistance wouldn't be needed. But as the minister insisted, here I am. You know how ministers are."

"And I suppose you'll go away in a few days and write a report about us," he stated with a suggestion of suspicious sarcasm in his voice. "No doubt trying to save your own skin."

Aha. The carabinieri grapevine was working with its usual efficiency. Bovolo had evidently heard Bottando's back was against the wall, and it didn't sound as though he was going to do much to help. She'd been afraid of that, but had prepared as best she could.

"I was hoping to ask you for a favour there," she said conspiratorially. "As you will be the man on top of the job, knowing exactly what was going on, I wondered— I know of course how busy you must be at the moment— if perhaps you might prepare it for me. Then we could avoid unnecessary errors . . ."

She smiled cutely once more and could see he'd taken the point. She was giving him the chance of virtually dictating what the report contained—or did not contain. A handsome offer, to her way of thinking. If that didn't cut the hostility level, nothing would. And, of course, she could always add on appendices and footnotes in Rome.

"Well," he said, "I'm not sure I approve of my department doing your job for you, but maybe it would be the best way of making sure all those interfering bureaucrats get an accurate account."

He nodded and brightened as he considered the choice words of praise for himself he could insert at strategic places.

"Yes," he said, very much happier. "Probably quite wise. But I don't want you hanging around here and getting in our way, you know. We're busy, understaffed and got better things to worry about than the murder of a foreigner who didn't have enough sense to look after herself."

Evidently not a man who could accept a gift with grace.

"I've no doubt," said Flavia, slightly perturbed, but pleased nonetheless that she appeared to be making some progress. "And I'd be more than happy to help in any way you suggest."

"Well, now," he said dubiously, clearly trying to think of something suitably unimportant, "I gather you're the educated type. Languages." He had a tone which implied this was a somewhat indecent attainment.

It was becoming a bit of an effort to keep up the vacuous smile. She hoped his manner would improve before her limited reserves of tolerance ran out entirely.

"Maybe you could talk to some of her colleagues?" he went on, paying no attention to the increasingly strained appearance of her facial muscles. "There's no point, of course, as we're after our man already. But it shows we've covered all angles. You could have a quick word with them, read over the documents, and go back to Rome tomorrow. You *are* going tomorrow, aren't you?" he added, half-suspecting a nasty complication.

"Yes. Or the day after. And I'd be happy to talk to them. But haven't you done that already?" she asked with some surprise.

"Oh, yes, of course," he said hurriedly. "Of course we have. Indeed. Detailed interviews. But it would do no harm to talk to them again, I'm sure. Keep you busy and out of our way."

"Well, in that case," she said briskly, dropping the smile on the grounds that it was doing little to advance her cause, "perhaps you could tell me what it's all about? The details down in Rome were very vague. Nobody there knows what happened or how. It would be a help to know. If, that is, you can spare the time."

Bovolo swivelled his fishy little eyes in her direction, not sure whether she was being polite or sarcastic. "Hmph," he snorted, gracious as ever. "Oh, well, why not? Might even help to hear the views of an outsider." He clearly thought nothing of the sort, but it was at least an attempt to be civil. Flavia tried to appear flattered.

"The victim's name," he began after a lengthy shuffle through the piles of papers on his desk, "was Louise Mary Masterson. She was fifty-eight, single, American citizen. She lived in New York and was keeper of Western Art at a museum there. One metre thirty-one high, good health. She joined the Titian committee eighteen months ago. This was to be her second session. They meet every year in Venice, at the taxpayers' expense. She arrived last Monday, and the meeting began on Thursday afternoon. She missed the first session but was there on Friday. Her death took place at, as far as the doctors can say, around 9:30 p.m. the same evening."

He spoke at a machine-gun pace, making it clear he had not the slightest interest in briefing her properly. Rather, he was making a valiant effort to spew out the maximum number of facts in the minimum time so he could get rid of the tiresome interloper as fast as possible. Flavia let him rattle away: so far, his recitation produced no details she felt like pursuing.

"The body was discovered in the Giardinetti Reali. That, by the way, is between the Piazza San Marco and the Grand Canal. She worked late in the Marciana library nearby and evidently went for a walk. All public transport was on a lightning strike and she may have been waiting for a taxi to come free. She was found in a greenhouse, stabbed seven times with a knife about ten centimetres long. Penknife. Swiss Army, maybe. That sort. Once in the throat, four times in the chest, once in the shoulder and once in the arm. None was fatal if she'd got help in time, but she was clearly dragged into the greenhouse to make sure she wasn't."

"So essentially she bled to death?"

"That's about it. Nasty way to go, I must admit. Quiet part of the world. Anywhere else, someone would have come across her in time. But that, unfortunately, is about it. None of her colleagues knows why she was there, and we've found no one who saw her in the garden. There weren't many people around because of that damnable strike. Murder, obviously. But by whom and why we don't know."

"Suspicions?"

"Oh, well, now. Suspicions, of course we have. More than that. It was certainly a simple robbery that got out of hand. There was no sign of rape, and her briefcase was missing. Not a Venetian crime obviously. A Sicilian, or some other sort of foreigner, no doubt."

Flavia decided to pass over this outrageous statement in silence. She, at least, did not consider her southern copatriots as foreigners, nor did she necessarily assume

that Venetians were incapable of murder. But there was
no need to ruffle feathers unnecessarily.

"No other hints or indications of what might have
taken place?" she asked.

Bovolo shrugged in the manner of someone who has
said his piece and is beginning to think further discussion
unnecessary. Still, they had an understanding—she
would not criticise, and he would humour her. He pushed
some papers across the desk for her to examine while he
continued talking.

"Those include as much as we know of her movements before her death. There is nothing at all out of the
ordinary. She didn't know anyone in Venice apart from
her colleagues; when not in the library she spent nearly
all her time on the Isola San Giorgio, either in her room,
eating or having meetings with the other members of the
committee. These," he continued, just as Flavia was
about to say that the details seemed very thin, "are photographs of the victim."

She looked intently, more out of a wish to seem professional than because she wanted to study them. Merely
glancing at them seemed almost an invasion of the
woman's privacy.

Even dead, she could see that Masterson had been a
fairly striking woman. A well-formed face, make-up
smudged. The clothes, dishevelled and bloodstained,
were evidently of high quality and, to her eyes, a little
conservative and severe. A close-up photograph of her
hand showed that it was curled round a bunch of flowers,
obviously grabbed hold of as she died. There was something else Flavia couldn't make out.

"What's this?"

"A lily," Bovolo said.

"Not the flower. This." She pointed to it.

"Crucifix," Bovolo said. "Gold. With a silver chain."

"That must be fairly valuable," she said. "I would have thought any robber would have taken it."

Bovolo shrugged noncommittedly. "Maybe, maybe not. She probably fought for it, that prompted him to kill her, he panicked and ran away. Or perhaps he really only wanted cash. It's safer, after all."

"What was in her case?"

"Professional papers, wallet, passport, that sort of thing, as far as we can work out." He handed over another list and a few xeroxes.

Flavia thought for a few seconds. She was very keen on instant impressions, mercurial guesses which always made Bottando adopt his long-suffering expression. He liked routine, and had tried over the years to convince her of its merits. Fair enough; he was a policeman and such procedure part of his job. She wasn't, and preferred imagination—which was as often right as Bottando's reliance on drudgery. Still, might as well show her devotion to method.

"No footprints, nothing like that?"

"It is a public garden," he said sarcastically. "Tourists tramp through all the time, treat the place like a dustbin. The shoreline was absolutely disgusting. Do you know how many empty cans and half eaten sandwiches my men had to collect?"

The last thing she wanted was to hear a long lecture on the nasty habits of tourists. Apart from the fact that Bovolo would probably want to ban all foreigners from the city, she lived in Rome and knew about the problem already.

"I just thought that if she'd been dragged into a greenhouse there would have been some prints nearby."

"Well, there weren't. Not recent ones anyway. Very

dry summer, hard ground. Hasn't rained for weeks. With a bit of luck it may any day now; we certainly need it. Of course, you can use up your time looking for yourself, if you think you can do a better job than our technical experts who have spent years examining this sort of thing . . ."

Flavia nodded in a way that hinted she might just do that. Not that she would, but it clearly irritated Bovolo, so was worth it.

There wasn't much to wrap her imagination around, it had to be said. But the photos of the woman interested her strangely. How much can you tell from photographs? Not much, admittedly, but Masterson looked as though she might have been a bit complicated. She dressed in a hard, no-nonsense style that Americans often prefer; there was none of the femininity that an Italian in her position might have manifested. Her face, also, had a determined edge to it. But there was an ambiguity there. Underneath was something softer, especially around the eyes, which contradicted the firm set of the mouth. Masterson gave the impression of someone trying to be more ruthless than was natural. She might have been quite pleasant had you managed to get through to her.

Flavia smiled, thinking how Bottando would have sniffed at this exposition, built as it was on nothing whatsoever. One glance at Bovolo was enough to convince her that he was a member of the same school of policework.

"You've worked out the whereabouts of all her colleagues, I imagine?" she asked.

Bovolo again reacted as though he didn't know whether she was being sweet or sarcastic, but suspected the worst. "Of course," he said primly, producing yet another sheaf of papers. He put his spectacles on the end of his nose and looked at the documents carefully, just in case they'd changed in the past five minutes.

"All perfectly reasonable accounts of themselves. And before you ask, we have also checked the clothes in their rooms and not found a single stain, bloody dagger or diary containing a full confession. Professors Kollmar and Roberts cancel each other out, as they were at the opera together. Dr Van Heteren was at dinner with friends near the railway station. Dr Lorenzo was at home, with servants and friends to testify to it. All of those four are staying on the main island, not at the foundation. That leaves Dr Miller."

"Tell me about him, then. I take it he had no witnesses?"

Bovolo nodded. "Yes. For a moment we also had high hopes there. However, he was on the island with no way of getting off it, because of the strike. He went into the kitchen just after ten to ask for some mineral water to wash down a sleeping pill, drank it down while talking to some of the staff, and went straight off to bed."

"But he is still the only one who has no one else to vouch for him at the time of the murder?"

"True. But the gatekeeper is prepared to swear no one left or arrived after about six o'clock. If he was on the island at ten, he was on it at nine. And in that case, he didn't kill this woman. Besides, all of them are most distinguished people with no possible motive. It was a very harmonious and scholarly operation, not a branch of the Mafia."

Flavia nodded thoughtfully. "So, having eliminated all her colleagues, you decide on a lone marauder."

Bovolo nodded. "And we'll stick with it, unless you have something else to suggest," he said with a don't-you-dare expression on his face.

"And what's that?" she asked, gesturing briefly at another envelope.

"This? Just her mail. Delivered to her room this morning and we picked it up. We thought it might have been
important, but it isn't. Take it if you like and check it
out. All art stuff."

She read through them briefly. Circulars, notes from
her museum, a letter from a photographic agency and a
couple of bills. Uninspiring. She put them all down in
the pile.

"Still," said Flavia, not really feeling comfortable, "it
seems odd to go to all that trouble to tear a gold crucifix
off her neck and then leave it behind. Was she a Catholic,
by the way?"

Bovolo shook his head. "Don't think so," he replied.
"You know what these Americans are like. All religious
fanatics, by the sound of them."

Another nation to cross off your list. Not a man with
a broad appreciation of the varieties of human culture.

"Take copies of these if you want," he said, gesturing
at the police files on the case with a sudden spurt of co-
operative generosity. "Not the photographs, obviously,
but anything else. As long as you give them back and
don't show them to anyone. They are confidential, you
know."

Why did she want all that miscellaneous debris? she
wondered after she'd shaken the inspector by his clammy
little hand and was walking slowly back to the Danieli.
Clearly Bovolo thought them useless, or he wouldn't
have allowed her to have them. She felt a slight glim-
mering of interest in this murder, despite Bottando's orders that she was not to get involved in any way. It was,
perhaps, the woman's face. There was no fright on it. It

was not the face of someone who'd died in the middle of a robbery. If there was any expression at all, it was determination. And indignation. That did not fit in at all with Bovolo's notion of a mugging somehow.

CHAPTER

3

Jonathan Argyll sat in a restaurant in the Piazza Manin, trying with mixed success to disguise both his upset at the message and his distaste for the messenger. It was not easy. He felt out of his depth, as usual, and was beginning to have a sneaking feeling that nature had not really designed him to be an art dealer, try as he might to earn an honest crust at the trade. He knew very well what he was meant to do. Ear to the ground to hear gossip in the trade, research in libraries to spot opportunities, careful approach to owners with an offer that, in theory, they leapt to accept. Easy. And he could do all of it pretty well, except for the last bit. Somehow the owners of pictures never seemed quite as ready to part with their possessions as the theory suggested they should be. Perhaps he just needed more practice, as his employer suggested. On good days, this is what he liked to think. On bad days, and this was one of them, he was more inclined to think it was not for him.

"But Signora Pianta, why?" he asked in an Italian flawed only by the distinct tone of weary desperation.

"If the terms weren't satisfactory, why on earth didn't she say so last month?"

The vulture-faced, mean-minded, vicious-looking old misery smiled in a tight and very unsympathetic fashion. She had a nose of quite alarming dimensions which curved round and down almost like a sabre, and he found himself increasingly fixated on the monstrous protuberance as the meal progressed and the quality of the conversation deteriorated. He had not especially noticed her singularly unappealing appearance before she demanded more money from him, but the shock had stimulated his senses. On the other hand, he had never liked dealing with her, and found the act of enforced gallantry increasingly difficult to sustain.

Very irritating. Especially as Argyll and the old Marchesa had hit it off well. She was a feisty, cunning woman with eyes still bright in her old and lined face, a bizarre sense of humour and a very satisfactory desire to unload some pictures. All was going nicely, more or less. Then she'd fallen ill, and it evidently made her cranky. Since her side-kick—companion, she liked to call herself—had taken over, the negotiations had lurched and sputtered. Now it appeared they were going to grind to a final halt.

"And I've already told you it is quite unnecessary. We are very experienced at this sort of thing."

Tiresome woman. She had spent the evening elliptically dropping bizarre hints, and eventually he had asked outright what on earth she wanted, apart from switching the deal to a percentage of the sale price rather than a lump sum. That he could deal with, although it would have been nice had she thought of it earlier.

It was the other little detail that upset him. Smuggle the pictures out, she said. Don't bother with export permits, official regulations and all that nonsense. Stick them in the back of the car, drive to Switzerland and sell them. Get on with it.

It was, of course, not that unusual. Thousands of pictures leave like that from Italy every year, and some of his less respectable colleagues in Rome made a tidy living as couriers. But, as he said firmly, Byrnes Galleries did not work like that. They went by the book, and were good at hurrying officialdom along. Besides, the pictures were relatively unimportant—family pictures, second-rate landscapes, anonymous portraits and the like—and there was no likelihood of any hitches. The price he had offered was not great, admittedly, but as much as they were worth. By the time they were paid for, transported to England, cleaned, prepared and sold, he and his employer would show a respectable profit. Worked out as a rate per hour for the amount of time he'd put in, he could probably earn more selling hamburgers in a fast food chain.

She was upset by his adamant refusal. In that case, she said, he must agree to pay all export taxes and registration fees. Whether she was serious or whether this was all a ploy to get him to agree to her request he did not know, but here he put his foot down.

"I've been through all the figures. We couldn't possibly sell the pictures, pay all the expenses and make a profit on this percentage. It's tantamount to calling the entire deal off."

Signora Pianta smiled and drank the coffee that Argyll, it seemed, was paying for. A meal designed to conclude an amicable deal was becoming an expensive waste of time. Initially, he had felt a certain sympathy for the woman, who had an unenviable position as companion

to the sharp-tongued Marchesa. It was now evaporating
fast.

"I'm very sorry," she said, not meaning it at all. "But
those were my instructions. And as we have now had
more interest in the pictures . . ."

Argyll was bewildered by this last comment. Who on
earth could be interested? Was he about to become involved in a bidding war for these things? If so, it certainly wasn't worth it. If he wasn't required occasionally
to provide Edward Byrnes in London with some pictures
as an exchange for his salary, he would pull out now and
go back to Rome.

"Oh, very well, then," he said reluctantly. "I'll think
about it and call you tomorrow."

Cool and professional, he thought. Don't allow yourself to be stampeded. Keep them guessing. Probably useless, mind you.

From there until the end of the meal he did his best to
remain calmly polite. He did all the right things; paid the
bill with much silent gnashing of teeth, helped her on
with her coat, escorted her out of the restaurant and was
kissing her hand—this always seemed to go down well,
even when it wasn't deserved—when he heard a slight
cough from someone standing just behind him in the
Campo.

He turned round, his bad mood dissipating as he recognised the woman standing there, resting with her
weight on her left leg, arms crossed and a look of amused
disdain on her face.

"What are you doing in Venice?"

"Not having as much fun as you, it seems," Flavia
replied.

Argyll, thrown into confusion as he was so easily by
almost anything unexpected, performed a flustered and

not very competent set of introductions. "Flavia di Stefano of the Polizia Art Squad in Rome," he concluded.

Pianta was not impressed. Indeed, she nodded coldly in the way of someone who did not consider the police respectable members of society, looked disapprovingly at her somewhat scruffy clothes—with particular emphasis on the unpolished brown boots—and then ignored her entirely. She thanked Argyll for the meal in a chilly sort of fashion, which bore no relation to how much it had cost, and walked off.

"Now there's a real charmer," Flavia remarked calmly as she went.

Argyll rubbed his nose in irritation and frustration. "Didn't seem to like you, did she? Don't take it personally. It may be because she's just been asking me to break the law. Besides, she doesn't like me either, and I've just paid for her dinner."

There was a long silence as he regarded her with a look of affection, which she always interpreted as one of discomfort. It was. He never really quite knew what to do with someone who was both emotionally turbocharged and also so calm and detached. Somehow the bits never seemed to fit together, or, to put it another way, they obviously did but he couldn't quite figure out where the joins were.

"What are you doing here, anyway?" he asked eventually. "I can't tell you how pleased I am to see you. A friendly face, you know."

"Thank you," she said formally, deciding that he had not been changed by his period of living in Rome. If he didn't understand her, at least it was mutual. His distant, if obvious, affection tended to confuse her. To her mind, he should either forget her or fling his arms round her. Either would do; but to manage neither seemed merely

indecisive. "I'm here for a couple of days on a case. Of
sorts. Not so interesting."

"Oh."

"What about you?"

"Wasting my time, it seems."

"Oh."

Another silence intervened. "Do you want to tell me
about it?" she said finally. "You look as though you
need to ventilate a bit."

He glanced sideways at her gratefully. "Yes," he said.
"I'd like that. You're starving, I imagine?"

She nodded fervently. "Yes. How do you know?"

"Lucky guess. Come on. I'll sit with you and have a
coffee. I love to watch a professional at work."

They walked into the restaurant again and sat down at
the same table he'd occupied before. "Same place, better
company," he said with an attempt at a charming smile
that was slightly more successful than the last.

While Flavia ploughed her methodical and diligent
way through much of the menu, Argyll gave a potted
history of his trials and tribulations. There was not much
she could say. The deal, it seemed to her, was off and
the only sensible thing to do was to go back to Rome.
But she tried to be optimistic. He should, she counselled,
hang around for a few days yet. You never knew, after
all. He could always go in for a bit of smuggling.

Argyll was properly shocked. "And you in the police
as well. I'm ashamed of you."

"Just an idea."

"No thanks. I will persevere for a few days by legal
means, then give up. What I'll do," he said with renewed
enthusiasm, "is try to get hold of the Marchesa direct
tomorrow. Go to the top. That might work."

He yawned, leant back in his chair and stretched.

"Enough of that. I'm sick of hearing about the damn things. Distract me. How's life in Rome these days?"

It was a pointed reminder that, though they lived in the same city, they hadn't seen much of each other recently. Argyll considered this distressing and Flavia also missed his company. But, as she explained, he'd been away, and she'd been busy. Times were tough, and the pressure was on while Bottando battled to save his department.

"In fact," she concluded, "the only reason I'm here is that everyone in Rome is all excited and Bottando is plotting."

"As usual, eh?"

They had different opinions on this; for the Englishman, Bottando's constant manoeuvrings revealed him as a consummate manipulator. Although he had enormous regard for the amiable Italian, he vaguely thought his time might more properly be spent catching criminals. Flavia, on the other hand, was of Bottando's view that efficiency was no use at all if the entire department was politicked into oblivion. She just wished he didn't involve her quite so often.

"It's serious this time," she said with a frown. "We've got a fight on our hands. I just hope he can get us out of trouble."

"I'm sure he will. He's extraordinarily well practised, after all. I suppose you're here on the Masterson affair that I've been reading about in the papers?"

Flavia nodded absently.

"Who done her in, then?"

"How should I know? The local police think she was mugged. Maybe she was. Not my business, anyway. I'm here simply to lend respectability, follow up anything arty and secure some tactical credit for the department at

a difficult moment. You don't, by any chance, know anything about the"—she paused to get out the letter and
check the name—"the *Agenzia Fotografica Rossi,* do
you?" she asked, switching the subject to something less
distressing.

"Eminently respectable, small business in Bologna
that keeps files of photographs. Often used by art historians gathering illustrations for books. Why?"

"No reason. Just that a letter from them for Masterson
arrived this morning. I thought I'd be diligent and check
it out. Something to put in the report," she said as Argyll
plucked it from her hand and read it.

It is not often that you can definitely say that you have
seen someone rock backwards in surprise, especially
when they are sitting in a chair. Nor do most people have
the opportunity of actually seeing someone change colour. Argyll, therefore, gave Flavia two new experiences
in a matter of seconds. She thought for a moment he was
about to fall off his seat. His pink complexion turned
pale, and then a mottled shade of green, as he read the
letter. Or, to be more accurate, as he goggled at it.

"What," he began in a tone which suggested he was
about to have hysterics. "What on earth are you doing
with this?" He had evidently seen something she had not,
so she craned round to examine it again.

"What's wrong with it?"

"Nothing," he replied. "Perfectly nice letter. A
model, no doubt. It's good to know the epistolary mode
is still with us in these days of mobile phones and elec-
tronics."

"Jonathan," she said with a warning tone in her voice.
He had a distressing tendency to head off into conversational cul-de-sacs when distracted or upset.

"She is asking for a photograph of a painting."

"Which they say they don't have. I know that."

"A portrait," he went on methodically, "belonging to the Marchesa di Mulino. Of no interest to anyone at all for nearly half a century. Except to me, and I have spent the last few months wasting my time trying to buy it. And just as I think all is going well, that Pianta horror says someone else is interested in buying. And now it appears that this other person is a woman who has been neatly knifed."

Flavia thought about that. She could see his concern, but didn't think it had much foundation. "It cuts down the competition," she said brightly.

He gave her a severe look. "A bit too literally, though."

"Who is this picture by?" she asked.

"No one."

"Someone must have done it."

"No doubt. But neither I nor anybody else knows who. Just Venetian school, circa 1500, or thereabouts. Very mediocre."

"Who is it a portrait of, then?"

"I don't know that, either," he said. "But it's probably a self-portrait."

"Not by Titian, I suppose?"

"Not a chance in ten billion. Titian could paint."

"What's it like?"

"Straightforward. Man with a big nose in robes, mirror, easel and palette in the background. Nothing exciting, really."

Flavia frowned mightily. "It does seem a bit of a co-incidence, I must say," she said with the clear reluctance of someone who sees her life being complicated unnecessarily.

"That struck me as well," he said moodily, reading

the letter again just to make sure he'd understood it properly. He had. "Very odd, in fact. It makes me fret." He leant back in his chair, crossed his arms defensively and frowned at her.

"Maybe you should ask some of her colleagues," he went on after a while. "Find out what she was up to. Maybe they could help. Has anyone talked to them?"

"Of course. The carabinieri here aren't total idiots. Not quite, anyway. But they mainly checked out alibis. Six members of the committee, one dead, five reasonable alibis."

"Hmph. Far be it from me to tell you how to do your job, but I think a chat with all of these people is called for. For my sake, at least."

"I'm going to. Not for your sake, though. And I don't have much time and I do have to be fairly discreet. After all, I was sent here specifically to be decorative, not to do anything."

"You are always decorative," said Argyll gauchely. "But I can't imagine you ever not doing anything. I couldn't come with you, could I, by any chance, perhaps?" He did his best to look winsome and the sort of person who could sit in an interview room without being noticed.

"You could not. Most improper. Relations with Bovolo are strained already and he'd blow his top. Besides, it's none of your business."

It was getting late, Flavia was tired and becoming irritable. She had a feeling she was going to need more time than she would be allowed on this case and, somewhat irrationally, she was beginning to resent Argyll for complicating matters with his infernal picture. Not that it was his fault, and it was unfair to snap at him. But she needed a good sleep urgently. So she called for the bill, paid and ushered him out into the chilly night air as fast as possible.

She stood outside the restaurant, hands in pockets, admiring the view and wondering which of the many little alleys would take her back to her hotel. She had a good sense of direction and was always distressed when it let her down. It always collapsed in a heap in Venice. Argyll stood opposite her, shifting his balance, as he usually did when considering matters.

"Right then," he ventured at last. "I'd better be off to my hotel. Unless you want me to guide you to yours . . ."

She sighed and smiled back at him. "I'd never get there," she said, missing the point. "It's quite all right, I'll manage. Come round tomorrow sometime and I'll fill you in." And she marched off, leaving a slightly aggrieved Argyll to wander around in circles until chance brought him to his own hotel.

CHAPTER

4

The next morning, Argyll was sitting in Flavia's bedroom armchair reading the newspaper. Knowing full well that her brusqueness of the night before would have vanished after eight hours of unconsciousness, he came round for breakfast to remind her to ask about his pictures. He'd spent some time thinking about it and was still a little worried.

He was in no great hurry to go about his own business. At the moment he didn't really have any. Instead, he was going to play a waiting game, he explained with what he hoped was the sly air of the seasoned professional. If they could be silly with him, the very least he could do was reply in kind.

''I want those pictures, but they're becoming complicated. My dearly beloved employer would never forgive me if I embroiled him in another little scandal,'' he said thoughtfully as he poured the last of the coffee.

In that he was undoubtedly correct. Sir Edward Byrnes was an easy-going man in many ways, but placed great store by his impeccable reputation as an honest prince of the international art business. Argyll's small but significant role in causing him to sell a fake Raphael to Italy's national museum nearly wrecked his career. Not that it was Argyll's fault—and he had sorted the mess out later, after a fashion—but it was a close run thing and a repetition would not go down at all well.

"How did you hear about these pictures, anyway? Another example of your art historical detective work?"

This was said with a light touch of sarcasm. Argyll's endeavours in this department had been painfully erratic in the past. He treated the comment with the disdain it deserved.

"Not exactly. The old lady wrote to Byrnes about six months ago. I think she reckoned the pictures were more valuable than they are. I was sent up to disabuse her of her notions and arrange the deal. Not my fault, you see."

He sighed at the troubles of life and drained his cup. "Want to spend some time looking at a few churches today? Or are you going off to be dutiful?" he asked as she pushed back her chair. She nodded.

" 'Fraid so. Committee member number one. Might as well get a move on. It's going to be a long day."

She looked, so the Englishman thought fondly, particularly gorgeous this morning. Loose hair, shining in the morning sunlight streaming through the window, open face, striking blue eyes. Hmph. He repressed his admiration, which he felt would not be appreciated at this time of the day. Alas, it seemed not to be appreciated at any time of day.

"And who's the lucky man?"

"Tony Roberts. I'm meeting him on the island. I thought I'd knock off the Anglo-Saxons first. Do you know anything about him?"

"Enough to know that he is not the sort of person to

be called Tony. Anthony, please. Much too dignified for diminutives. Like referring to Leonardo da Vinci as Lenny.''

"What's he like?''

"Depends on who you listen to. On the one hand there's the fan club. Great man, major contribution to scholarship. Gentleman and connoisseur. You know the sort of thing. Perfect manners and absolute professional integrity. A latter-day saint. On the other hand there is the view that, however charming, he is really a pompous old goat. That, admittedly, is an opinion mainly held by those who have not benefited from his vast patronage network.''

"But is he any good?''

Argyll shrugged again. "Again, opinions vary. His book on Venetian art competitions is generally accepted as a revolution in methodology. The less enthusiastic add that he's done damn all since. And twenty years is a long time to live on your reputation. As for me, I don't know. I've never met him. He is an avid collector of pictures and as far as I know he pays his bills. What more could anybody want?''

The fondazione Cini is another name for the old monastery of San Giorgio Maggiore, a sixteenth-century masterpiece by Palladio taken over by the state and converted into an upmarket conference centre. It is the sort of place where you hold international summits, or conferences for people who need to be impressed. Nothing, it seemed, was too good for the historians of Venice's most successful painter and every year a well-appointed conference room, a suite of convenient bedrooms, telephones, fax machines, photocopiers, as well as a bevy of cooks and housemaids, were set aside for the Titian committee's exclusive use.

If anything should have focused their minds on the task at hand, quarters on the island should have done the trick. Facing San Marco, with the Salute on the left, the stone, terracotta and brick of the buildings positively glowed in the fading and ever rarer autumn sunlight, ample proof on its own that Venice was one of the great wonders of the world.

Flavia stood on the vaporetto and watched, entranced, as the island drew nearer. Her face was lightly tanned from the summer, her long, fair hair streamed backwards in the breeze. Had Argyll seen her standing like that, legs slightly apart to keep her balance, hands thrust into the pockets of her jeans, a slight frown on her forehead from the sun, he would have been even more lost in admiration than at breakfast. But he would never have found any way of telling her, and Flavia was incapable of divining what he was thinking.

"Too late," said the guardian brusquely as she approached, gesturing at the timetable that announced the building was closed to tourists until noon. It was now only ten. She fished out her identification card and announced herself as a member of the police. He examined it carefully, back and front, glancing up at her suspiciously as he read.

"From Rome, eh?" he said, suggesting strongly that she should be ashamed of herself.

"The Titian committee," she said severely. "Where do I find its meeting rooms?"

"Oh," he said knowingly. "That lady that got herself killed, is it?" He said it in a way which implied that it had been the American's own fault. Everybody seemed to do that.

"That's right. Did you know her?"

"A bit. Not much. Some people take the time to stop and talk, even know my name. Not her. She did chat to my wife, though. She says she was pleasant, not that they had much to talk about. My wife," he added, heading off at an apparently unrelated tangent, "cleans the rooms here, you know."

"Really?" said Flavia, taking the hint about conversation. "How long has she been doing that for?"

"Oh, years, now. The year of the flood she started." Flavia tried to remember. 1966? October? Something like that. Not that it mattered. "Eight hours a day. And she helps wash up in the evenings. And do you know how much she's paid?"

Probably very little, but she had no time to listen to complaints, however well justified. "Doesn't seem very busy now, though. There are only the historians here at the moment, aren't there?"

He grudgingly admitted that it was pretty slack. "Doesn't mean this place is easy to keep clean," he countered.

"No?"

"No. Shoddy, that's what it is. Looks nice, I grant you. But shoddy. Can't do anything properly round here these days."

She was on the verge of asking if by chance he was related to an old gondolier she knew. "Workmanship. Hah. International conference centre, so-called. Can't even stop the roof leaking. That's because all the contracts—you know." He glanced at her slyly and put his finger to his nose to imply dirty dealings in high places. She knew what he meant. He was probably right.

"Do you know, last week, there was water coming in? Would you credit it? Puddles of it in the corridors. Which my wife had to clean up even after her shift had ended. Faulty roofing. Lets in the rain. Lucky none of it got into the bedrooms, or this lot would have complained. They always do, you know. Never satisfied, some people.''

"There must be some interesting people who come here,'' she ventured desperately, hoping to get him off the subject so she could find out where the meeting room was.

"Interesting? Don't know about that. Odd, certainly. Some funny people we've had here. Don't know that I approve. They call themselves respectable, you know.''

"Are they not?''

"Some of them. Some I wouldn't let into my house. Of course, I don't want to judge them. Live and let live, I suppose, and people always do get a bit frisky in Venice, if you know what I mean.''

She had some idea.

"Take that lady that got herself killed,'' he continued. The twinkle in his eye told Flavia he knew quite well he was playing with her.

"She didn't get herself killed. Someone murdered her.''

"That's what I said,'' he replied, clearly thinking she was being pedantic.

Flavia sighed. "Take her how?'' she asked.

"Is that for me to say? All I know was, that she was a bit of a night-owl, that one.''

"You mean she worked late?''

The guardian snickered, and rubbed his red, drinker's nose with the back of his hand. "Work, it might have been.'' He leered at her in a peculiarly repulsive fashion.

"Perhaps she had friends in?''

This he found a great joke and looked at Flavia as though he'd found a soul-mate at long last. "Oh, yes,'' he gurgled. "Friends, eh?" He cackled away merrily.

Flavia sighed once more. It was always hard to deal with gossips. On the one hand, they had an incurable urge to tell you what they knew, on the other there was the long-standing unwillingness to say anything to the police at all. The result was often such a series of elliptical hints, designed to satisfy both imperatives.

"Tell me about the others," she began, and promptly abandoned the question when she saw the distrustful expression taking over again. "I assume your wife was in the kitchen with Dr Miller on Friday evening?"

This he could answer. No harm in exonerating people. "Yes. He came to the kitchen from the laundry-room to ask for some water at about half ten. We had a little chat. Very considerate, charming man."

"And he didn't leave the island at any time?"

"Oh, no. He was here, all right. No public transport and if he'd taken a taxi I would have seen it. And before you ask," he said conclusively, "there are no private boats here at the moment he could have taken."

"You have to open the door to let people in after hours?"

"No. People are given their own keys. But, as I say, I was on duty from six to midnight and would have seen anybody coming or going. No one did."

That seemed pretty conclusive. After a brief pause to note the conversation down, she made her way through to the second cloister in search of the committee's rooms. Yet again, her sense of direction abandoned her and she ended up at what seemed to be a service entrance somewhere at the far end of the building. With a curse, she turned round and began again, this time finding herself in the kitchens.

Third time lucky, she hit the right floor and made her

way along a corridor, with doors that were clearly the
rooms of those members of the committee who wanted
the free accommodation. Only Miller and Masterson did,
it seemed. The rest preferred to make their own arrangements.

Whatever the quality of the workmanship in the roofs,
the meeting rooms seemed more than adequate for their
purpose. Lashings of oak panelling, a handsome ceiling
painting of a suitably religious nature, even though the
large number of naked bodies swirling around seemed
scarcely designed to keep the old monks' minds on their
devotions, along with all the normal equipment of modern conference centres—comfortable armchairs, *settecento* tables, Venetian glassware, Flemish tapestries, that
sort of thing.

And, in the middle, sitting upright at the end of the
long wooden table evidently used for meetings, was Professor Roberts. She was sure it was him, although there
were three people in the room; whereas the oldest man
very much looked the part of the Great Man of his profession, complete with silver hair, tweed jacket, aquiline
nose and aristocratic bearing, the others could never pass
as great anythings.

Professor Roberts would, on balance, have approved
of Argyll's brief summary of him as being largely accurate. He was a man who had learned early in life that
you cannot arrange matters so that everybody loves you
simultaneously. That being the case, the best you can do
is to ensure that those who dislike you can do you no
harm.

This golden rule he had followed since he had for-
mulated it about a quarter of a century previously, but it
should not be taken as the mark of an unpleasant man.
Far from it. Roberts had a great reputation for his civility,

his hospitality and his grace. An entire generation of young scholars referred to him in awed tones because of his immense knowledge and his kindness to students. As Argyll had said, he valued his reputation for integrity, and worked hard to preserve it.

Flavia's identification was, of course, correct. Roberts introduced himself in the way of someone conferring a favour, and brusquely introduced the other men—who seemed very much less at ease—as his colleagues on the committee, Dr Miller and Dr Kollmar. From there on he made it clear that he was the one who was going to do all the talking, not that the others showed the slightest sign of wanting to intervene.

Flavia went through all the standard preliminaries, paying attention more to the way he answered rather than to what he actually said. The facts she knew already: he'd been on the committee since it was founded, held a chair in England, had published this, that and the next thing. All standard and uninteresting. She also sneaked a look in her notes to remind herself about the other two. Kollmar a German and on the committee since it was founded. Miller another American, more junior, job at a college in Massachusetts, where he was due to come up for tenure next year.

"Coffee?" Roberts asked, gesturing at an eighteenth-century silver pot in the corner.

While he was pouring, she examined the pile of notes on the desk. There was nothing else to do; the others didn't seem to want to take up the conversational slack. There was one book, and she picked it up.

"This is Masterson's, isn't it?" she said, reading the cover.

Roberts gave her a penetrating look from behind the coffeepot, and then relaxed. "That's right. I borrowed it from her on Wednesday. I needed to refer to some parts for an article I am writing. There are some excellent passages in it.''

A bit of a backhanded compliment, she thought. It looked deadly dull stuff to her. Still, part of her job as an artistic expert. She'd get Argyll to have a flip through; it would do him good to read something serious for once. She asked if she could take it, as it should be with Masterson's other possessions for return to her next of kin.

Roberts was disapproving. ''I would much rather you didn't,'' he began. ''I still need it.''

Flavia suggested that she thought Masterson's murder might be slightly more urgent a matter and he took the hint, reluctantly but with grace.

''But of course. Extraordinarily selfish of me. I confess I still can't believe she is dead. But do take it. I can survive without, I'm sure.''

There was a scuffle from Kollmar, the first real sign of life the man had shown. He was perhaps ten years younger than Roberts, but seemed half a decade older. He looked as though life had not been hugely kind in its dealings with him. Short and wiry, with a pinched face lined by years of preoccupation and worry. He was scruffily but passably dressed and Flavia instantly put him down as one of life's victims. Not, of course, she reminded herself with an upsurge of professionalism, that this implied innocence. Or even that he was pleasant.

''I was wondering—'' he began.

''Oh, indeed. Indeed,'' Roberts interrupted as he came over with Flavia's coffee cup. ''Thoughtless of me. Please do go. I'm sure that will be all right. Perhaps you can get the results round to me this evening? I really need that information quickly.''

He turned his attention to Flavia. ''Dr Kollmar is in a

great hurry to get to the library to do some work. That won't cause you any problems, I'm sure.''

It clearly wouldn't make any difference if it did, she thought as the German picked up his briefcase and scurried off. In fact, she was a touch irritated, both because she would now have to go and see the man separately, and because Roberts had so effortlessly taken charge and organised matters for his own benefit. She felt sure that all Kollmar was going to do before he was interrupted and sent off was to ask for a cup of coffee himself. Still, interesting. There was no doubt who was the head of this little band of brothers.

That little task accomplished, Roberts handed over her coffee and sat down once more, arranging himself into the same pose of authoritative elegance she had noticed when she first walked in.

''It occurred to me to wonder,'' he murmured quietly, ''which one of us you suspect. Am I, for example, on your list?''

He said it in a way clearly designed to indicate that he considered the idea ludicrous, but Flavia thought she could just detect a flicker of concern, deep below the surface. Far more obvious was the anxiety that Miller demonstrated at a remark that was probably designed only to catch Flavia off-balance. Miller was very much upset. In fact, he looked as though he was about to be sick.

''What makes you think that we suspect any member of the committee? Surely Commissario Bovolo has told you—''

''About his Sicilian. Yes, and of course that's comforting, even if it is nonsense.''

''Why do you think that?''

''Louise was an American. She'd lived for years in

New York and knew very well how to take care of herself. She was a very determined and confident woman. Not the sort of person who'd be caught like that.''

''Does this mean you would like to implicate one of your colleagues?'' she asked.

''Good heavens, no,'' he said, evidently shocked at the very thought of doing something quite so vulgar. ''I have not the slightest idea who killed her. But it occurred to me that you might wonder if the killer may have had a better reason than theft.''

''Which you did not.''

Roberts inclined his head. ''Which I did not. Nor, I must add, did anyone else I know. In my case it was quite the opposite, in fact. I rather saw her as my own protégée.'' He smiled as he spoke. ''Although, of course, Louise was much too proud and independent ever to accept such a subservient role with anyone. Which was why we had our differences of opinion that, alas, were not resolved before her death.''

''What was she like?''

''How do you mean?''

''As a historian, a person, a colleague. Liked? Admired? What?''

''That, of course, depends on who you ask,'' Roberts said, unknowingly echoing Argyll's own words about him. ''As far as her work went, she showed very great promise indeed.''

Again, a touch of condescension towards a woman in her late thirties. ''Personally,'' he went on, ''I never had any cause to regret recommending her for membership. She was briefly a pupil of my great friend Georges Bralle, and that was more than good enough for me.''

Miller gave a faint snort, and Flavia looked at him

enquiringly. Roberts, she noted, also gazed at him, although with a more disapproving air.

"Well," Miller began reluctantly, evidently uncertain whether he was about to step out of line and still not entirely recovered from the nasty shock that Roberts had given him with his opening remarks, "that's not exactly true. She was at Columbia with me and took off for a year to live in Paris. She had enough family money to do that sort of thing. She joined Bralle's classes, and came back a year later with a reference from him. On the strength of that she got her job and never looked back."

Flavia noted the comment, which didn't exactly brim over with affection and regret, but decided to ignore it for the time being. She turned her attention back to Roberts. "She joined about eighteen months ago, is that right?"

He nodded again. "Yes. Because Dr Bralle retired. Do you know the story of the committee, by the way?"

She shook her head.

"It was formed as a sort of private venture twelve years ago. By Bralle, with myself and Kollmar. We were both the great man's pupils. Van Heteren joined a few years after, Miller here about five years ago. We burrowed away as best we could and then we were, so to speak, nationalised."

"I beg your pardon?"

"Taken over by the state. We were working on our own, on a shoestring and basically couldn't afford it any more. Then the Italian Arts Ministry decided it wanted to fund a prestige project and offered us vast subsidies and official status. I negotiated the arrangement, which came into operation a few years ago."

"Very nice for you."

He didn't seem so grateful.

"The money was very useful. But a lot of bureaucracy comes with it, of course. Bralle didn't like the idea much and decided to retire. Naturally, an Italian had to be appointed to the committee—Dr Lorenzo, who joined us two years back. As we had more money and the pointed desire of the Arts Ministry for something to show for it, we had to step up the workpace and settled on Dr Masterson to help."

There was something in his tone which suggested that the changeover wasn't quite the smooth and amicable operation that was laid out. "And Masterson didn't turn out as well as you thought?"

Roberts paused to weigh his words. Flavia sensed that he was trying to fine-tune his message—maliciousness with the appearance of objectivity. She found herself not liking him as much. "*I* had no complaints," he said with careful emphasis.

"But . . . ?"

"Let us say that she was fairly young and inexperienced. She would, of course, have settled in and become indispensable once she'd got the hang of how we proceeded. Some of my colleagues, I think, had less faith than I did." It was extraordinary the way he talked as if Miller wasn't even in the room.

"You don't think you made a mistake in recommending her, in other words."

Roberts was not the sort of man who ever admitted to making a mistake. Either that, or he believed in loyalty. "Goodness, no. She brought conscientiousness and enthusiasm, but she did need a bit more practice in the technique of committee work. And, of course, she didn't always express herself as tactfully as she might have."

All these little hints. Why on earth could people not

be direct? Discretion was one thing, but it could be carried too far.

"What exactly do you mean, Professor?"

"Well. To take one example. I might as well mention it as you are bound to hear the tale eventually. Do you, by any chance, know how we go about our task here?"

Flavia shook her head. She'd had to master a considerable amount of detail in the past twenty-four hours; the minutiæ of art historical collaboration was not amongst the information given high priority. It was, unfortunately, an excuse for a major diversion.

As Roberts explained it, their method was very simple. Each member of the committee was allotted a picture to study, either alone or in collaboration, and wrote a report. This was discussed at their annual meetings and the committee then voted to assign the work a rank. "A" meant a genuine Titian, "B" was uncertain and "C" meant definitely not genuine. Those deemed "A" were then subjected to further scientific tests to check for mistakes. The individual reports and assessments were then slowly accumulated and produced in a series of expensive, glossily illustrated volumes.

Flavia became increasingly surprised as he explained. "Do you really mean to say that most of you vote on whether a picture is genuine or not without even seeing it?"

"Yes. In most cases it is quite unnecessary. Titians are spread all over the globe and we can't all go running around looking at each and every one. Besides, since we accepted state money we have been put under steady pressure to produce what the ministry likes to call value for money. It's this new and competitive age we live in, as Dr Lorenzo keeps on telling us. An appalling state of affairs."

"So how long do you spend on each picture?"

"Examining it, you mean? Oh, that depends. Often a couple of hours is enough."

"That's ridiculous. It seems very rushed to me. This is meant to be a definitive study, isn't it?"

Roberts shrugged. "I assure you it is more thorough than most such projects. We have several hundred pictures to study and we are all getting older. The point I was getting at is that at Louise's first meeting Dr Kollmar recommended that a picture in a Milanese collection be rated "C." It was a picture I had examined, with Dr Kollmar doing the archival research. I had no definite opinion one way or the other, but Dr Kollmar concluded the documentary evidence was inadequate. Everybody agreed to accept his judgement, except Louise. She had also agreed initially, then turned round the next day and caused a fuss."

"Why?"

"I think it was mainly her enthusiasm. But it was taken too far and people were beginning to get very ill-humoured. That always strikes me as regrettable. What is the point of this project if it turns into personal battles for power? I did my very best to persuade her to leave off, for everybody's sake."

"And did you succeed?"

"Partly. I did at least persuade her to keep quiet about it. It was all very tiresome. Louise was reluctant to agree and was somewhat sharp with me, as I mentioned. I have a high regard for Kollmar's work and am prepared to accept what he recommends. The picture is just an oil sketch for a religious painting. Subject uncertain. Stylistic evidence dates it to the early sixteenth century. Louise implied that the work was not done correctly."

"That doesn't seem unreasonable. After all, you don't

want any mistakes," Flavia ventured, drawing a frown from Roberts.

"Of course not. I didn't mind myself, but Dr Kollmar was upset. He thought it a little improper of her to start querying people's work at her first meeting. However, you will have to ask him. It would be most inappropriate for me to describe his reactions for him."

"And what were Masterson's conclusions?"

"I don't know. She was due to deliver her paper yesterday. I suppose it was in her case that was stolen."

"Is it possible to reach an incontestable conclusion over something like this?"

It was an invitation to discourse that he was not likely to turn down. Roberts leant back in the chair, crossed his legs and put the tips of his fingers together, for all the world as though he was instructing one of his more backward students. "Well, now," he began. "You must remember that Titian was undoubtedly one of the greatest geniuses of the Renaissance. So in theory it should be possible to isolate the spark of brilliance that must be in all his works. However, even geniuses of his stature do not spring forth, so to speak, ready formed . . ."

Flavia was regretting the request already. The man spoke as though every word began with a capital letter, and a certain glitter in his eye suggested someone settling down for a long haul. She could not even begin to see how an exposition on Titian's niftiness with the paintbrush was relevant. But she had asked for it, so she relaxed with as much good grace as possible and tried to appear both patient and interested.

Roberts was rabbiting on about the young Titian—how he started in the studio of Bellini, then came under the influence of Giorgione. "They painted the Fondaco dei Tedeschi in Venice together, as I'm sure you know."

Flavia nodded with slight irritation. She knew it very well, and rather resented being treated like a total ignoramus.

"They were great friends for a while, but the friendship ended when Titian stole his teacher's mistress and stumped off to work in Padua in 1510. Giorgione died the same year, of a broken heart and the mistress died of plague. End of story. The point is that Titian went through a lot of influences—he painted in the style of Bellini, then of Giorgione—and only gradually developed his own distinctive mannerisms."

"I know that. But so what?" she said shortly, hoping that a degree of brusqueness might get the man back to the more immediate, if less tasteful, present.

"The significance of my little lecture is that the style of his paintings in this early period alter as Titian experimented, and learnt and matured. This puts a question mark over possible pictures unless there is documentary evidence proving authorship. And Kollmar decided—he is the expert in this department—that this doesn't exist. I suppose Louise reckoned she could prove Titian's authorship in other ways."

"And do you have any further information about what might have happened on Friday evening?" she said, grateful that he had finally stopped and hoping to steer him into more orthodox and productive areas of police enquiry.

"None whatsoever. The first I heard that anything was wrong was when I got to the island on Saturday morning and found Lorenzo in a panic and police all over the place. On the day in question I can think of nothing of interest. We met in the morning, I had lunch with Dr Miller to discuss tactics for his forthcoming tenure dispute at his college in America—I'm one of his referees—

and we had another session in the afternoon until about three. Then I went to get the tickets, rest and change for the opera. All perfectly normal.''

"Did you talk to her much?"

He shook his head. ''Only over routine matters of business, and then not a great deal. She missed the first day's meeting, which caused some bad feeling; went sight-seeing in Padua, so Miller here told me. She seemed in one of her more determined moods, but said nothing noteworthy at all. Unusually quiet for her, in fact.''

There seemed little else that was worth pursuing at the moment. She was beginning to find Miller quite inter-esting, but it was clear that she was not going to get a clear run at him as long as Roberts was within half a mile or so. Not that this was necessarily suspicious; all it meant was that Roberts liked to dominate proceedings so much it was difficult for anyone else to get a word in. She wondered what committee meetings were like with him around.

So she stood up to go, and was gratified to see that the movement broke up the little tête-à-tête as well. Miller announced that he was going to go over to the swimming pool for a dip.

"Splendid," commented Roberts a little waspishly. "I always think that the United States is the last outpost of the Renaissance man. *Mens sana*, eh, Miller?"

Miller smiled dutifully, if half-heartedly, at a little joke he had probably heard several times already, and muttered that he found swimming very helpful in times of stress. This, he added, was a time of stress.

"Indeed. But I hope it won't distract you from other matters. Go and see Dr Kollmar and remind him that I need that archive material by this evening. It's most important if I am to get this lecture of mine finished in time.''

An order is an order. Evidently both Miller and Kollmar were used to carrying them out. She lurked in the corridor outside Miller's room until he emerged, clasping flippers, towels and the other impedimenta of the swimmer. He was clearly an enthusiast; little stickers on the bag he carried commemorated a whole series of swimming meets that, presumably, he had attended over the years. Physical fitness is a wonderful thing, no doubt, but Flavia, who spent the first hour of her day smoking furiously and drinking the strongest coffee she could make, and whose idea of swimming equipment was a deck-chair and suntan lotion, did not entirely approve.

''I suppose you want to give me a good grilling without Professor Roberts answering all the questions for me?'' he said flatly as they walked together down the staircase and headed for the jetty.

''Not quite the way I'd put it, but close enough,'' she replied. They had switched to English. With Roberts they had spoken only Italian and Miller's only interjection had been a little fractured.

''How did Masterson get on the committee?'' she asked, thinking that Miller's account might vary a little from what his colleague had said.

Miller shrugged as he clacked down the stone steps. Flavia looked down. Although dressed in jeans and a T-shirt, Miller had, through some strange and very un-Italian quirk of fashion consciousness, put on black dress shoes. Strange people, these Americans.

''Don't think I'm down on her, or anything,'' he said. ''She was very accomplished and highly motivated. But she was not an obvious choice.''

''It wouldn't be because her work was good?'' Flavia

again noticed her wish to defend the poor dead woman from the doubts and criticisms of her male colleagues. She was beginning to identify with this corpse far too much.

For the first time since she'd met him, Miller was genuinely amused. "Heaven forbid," he said. "That is rarely enough on its own. She was not, after all, a specialist on Titian; her research was on Renaissance iconography generally."

"So Masterson wrote, and did her job at the museum and worked with the committee as well?"

"No one ever accused her of being a slouch. She was always conscientious. Perhaps she published too much? I don't know. A bit thin, some of her stuff. And not nearly as original as she liked to make out, I know that. No, I'm fairly certain she was appointed simply because she was a woman."

"Meaning?" she said, bristling at the remark. If there was one thing she hated . . .

"Obvious, isn't it? All these projects have to have a woman on them these days, to show they're open-minded and progressive. Lorenzo is very keen on that, which is why he allowed the appointment. He couldn't think of anyone else. She was very lucky, considering."

"Considering what?"

"Considering that Lorenzo and Roberts don't exactly see eye to eye over anything. Poor Roberts. He thought he was doing everybody a favour by organising the state grant. We certainly needed the money. Then Bralle retires and Roberts gets lumbered with Lorenzo, who immediately tries to take over. If Louise hadn't been a woman there would have been no chance of her being appointed."

"What was she like?" asked Flavia, launching once

more into her favourite area of enquiry and feeling that any more of these needling remarks would make her boil over. They had arrived at the jetty and she saw the vaporetto approaching. A brief pause followed as she ran to the kiosk to get a ticket.

"I liked her well enough," he said with a somewhat excessive attempt to be fair when she finally returned with the requisite piece of paper. "A good enough colleague. Not easy to get to know; sharp tongue. Didn't suffer fools gladly."

"You weren't lovers?" she asked. Nothing like the direct approach. The question was followed by a long pause.

"Good God, no," he said eventually with a faintly ironic smile. "Louise was a human iceberg. She did have a thing with Van Heteren, I gather. He was very smitten indeed. The mind boggles, frankly. But he got in the way of her work so was given his marching orders. He was not happy about it. His own fault. I did warn him, not that he listened to me."

"What's the point of this committee? Personally, I mean. What do you all get out of it?"

He thought for a second. "Different people, different reasons. I like to think that everybody is mainly motivated by the love of scholarship, but sometimes, when I see the wrangling and bitching that goes on, my faith wanes a little. Roberts and Lorenzo both like controlling things, in their very diverse ways. Kollmar is genuinely, almost naïvely, scholarly. He wouldn't know a political gambit if one came and stood on his foot. Van Heteren just likes having a good time at other people's expense. Louise, I think, was motivated mainly by ambition."

Not a great testimonial to any of them, really, she thought as the boat chugged its way across the five-hundred-yard opening of the Grand Canal on the way to the Piazza San Marco. You could see quite clearly, she thought absently, the gardens where Masterson had been stabbed. "And you?" she said, bringing herself back to the matter at hand.

He smiled at her. "I suppose you think I'm being hard. So I am. But I don't let myself off lightly. In my case I'm motivated above all by the need for security. For me, it's something that will help when I come up for tenure, which is why I feel so jumpy at the moment."

"I beg your pardon?"

"Nervous. After a few years universities in the US have to decide whether to chuck you out or keep you for good. No laughing matter, with the job market being what it is. If I don't keep this post, I'll never get another. Joining this committee was almost providential. It gained me the support of Roberts as a referee and gave me a lot of prestige. Then Louise is murdered and being associated with the committee becomes less reputable. Especially if the finger of suspicion starts pointing in our direction. Who'd want to give tenure for life to a possible murderer?"

She saw why he was tense.

"Is Roberts right? Do you really suspect one of us?"

Flavia felt sudden sympathy for him. "No," she replied reassuringly. "No reason to. Your alibis are all impeccable. All I'm doing is sorting out loose ends."

"And the chances of finding the person responsible?"

"Not good, if it was just a random attack. But we should dredge up enough to convince everybody that none of you was responsible. I hope so at least. I wouldn't want this to damage anybody else."

The boat lurched to a halt at San Marco and they queued and shuffled their way off, just managing it before the swarm of people trying to get on board began pushing forward and blocking the gangway. Flavia straightened her clothes after the effort.

"Nice to have met you," he said as she prepared to leave. "And thanks for the reassurance. I appreciate it."

"Enjoy your swim."

Miller was uncertain whether she was also making fun of him. "I find it very relaxing," he said defensively. "Louise, in the same circumstances, would have spent the time in a library reading the latest publications. Maybe that's why she was always more successful than me."

Flavia shrugged. "Maybe that's why she's dead," she added. It was merely a good exit line, without any conscious meaning, but it threw Miller into confusion. As she marched off, she glanced at her watch. Time for lunch, to stoke up on the calories before starting on the next candidate.

CHAPTER

5

Flavia was developing a picture of Louise Masterson as the very epitome of the American professional woman. Tough, businesslike, efficient. Tenacious and thorough. A hard worker, as well; witness the fact that she was in the library until closing time the night of her murder. She had then walked out of the exit into the piazzetta, gone along the quayside and into the Giardinetti Reali. There she had evidently encountered her murderer. But so far, no personality. There must have been more to her than the driven, hard-working automaton that Roberts and Miller had described, and she rather hoped that the next interview would help flesh out the picture. That is, if she was right in assuming that the visitor so salaciously alluded to by the porter at the foundation was indeed Hendrick Van Heteren.

Van Heteren, as his name suggested, was Dutch. She had prepared herself for a nervy little man who could twitch and fidget in six languages simultaneously. The impression, half-formed though it was, was about as inaccurate as it was possible to imagine.

He was enormous. Not fat, just enormous. About the
same size as the isle of Elba, give or take an acre. Lots
of hair which stuck out as though he had recently been
electrocuted and a beard that was trimmed every three
days with a hedge cutter. A crippling handshake, a wide,
pockmarked face which was quite remarkably ugly although oddly friendly at the same time. An open, Techni-
coloured shirt that was in striking contrast to the dullness
of his eyes, the muted way he greeted her and the distracted way he talked. She tried the silent observation
treatment to soften him up and found that he stared morosely back, so she abandoned it hurriedly for more con-
ventional interrogatory methods.

The tiny apartment he occupied—it belonged to a
friend and its main advantage was that he did not have
to spend his time in Venice surrounded by art historians,
he confessed gloomily—was so small it was a minor miracle he ever managed to get in. To call it a mess would
be an understatement. Unmade bed, socks all over the
floor, several dozen books scattered around, every cup
and mug and plate and pan in the place dirty and over-
flowing from an aromatic sink. She liked it. This was her
sort of domesticity. But she wondered how such a person
got on with the fastidious Roberts, the upright Miller and
the evidently pedantic Kollmar.

So she asked him, that seeming the most direct way
of satisfying her curiosity.

He smiled half-heartedly, acknowledging the validity
of the question. She was struck by his very obvious sadness. It was interesting because it was so rare. Van Heteren was the only person so far who seemed genuinely
upset about Masterson's death. She warmed to him for
that, demonstrating again the partiality that made her feel
inadequate in dealing with this case.

"You don't think we're all birds of a feather, right?" He said in English. He spoke good, but not perfect Italian, and Flavia's Dutch was notable for its non-existence. So they compromised on English, which the Italian spoke well and Van Heteren spoke vividly, if waywardly.

"I suppose you're right," he continued. "Bralle—I imagine you've heard of him by now—is a very charming, very accomplished man. But a manipulator. You might say he taught Roberts everything he knew," he concluded archly.

"What does that mean?"

"Well, now. What do I mean? It's difficult to describe the old man really. He is a truly great historian, but he believes in keeping people off-balance. Little pinpricks, just to make you feel insecure. He plays favourites, so that everybody always feels someone else is better. He makes snippy comments behind people's backs; you know the sort of thing. He has little nicknames for people, often funny, in a cruel sort of way. He always called me Pigpen, why I don't know. Kollmar he referred to as the Invisible Man. And so on. You see what he was getting at, or at least you will when you meet Kollmar, but it wasn't always very nice. I think he chose us deliberately so we wouldn't get on all that well. So that only he could keep the operation going."

"But he's gone, and the committee survives."

"For the time being, true. But that's another story. Roberts pulled off his conjuring act of getting a grant from the Italian state. There's nothing quite like money for making people put up with each other, even though Bralle didn't like the idea at all. Although how long they'll manage to keep it up is uncertain. Sooner or later someone is going to be knifed in the back."

His face fell still further as he realised that his choice

of metaphor was not, perhaps, entirely ideal. Flavia
slipped this comment alongside all the others she'd heard
that day. Certainly, this committee did not seem to be a
harmonious bunch at all. Roberts and Lorenzo didn't get
on, Miller didn't think much of Van Heteren, Masterson
was after Kollmar. Dear me. Not a good advert for the
contemplative life. Even Bottando would have his work
cut out dealing with this lot.

She noted it all down in her little book, and got down
to the routine, guiding Van Heteren through the details
of his statement. All checked. He'd been with friends
until past midnight, come straight back home and gone
to bed. He was covered for the time of Masterson's death,
as were they all. More's the pity. She still didn't like the
Sicilian option.

"Was she religious, do you know?"

He looked puzzled at the question. "Not really. She
wore a little gold crucifix. Never took it off. But it was
a present from her grandmother; it had no religious significance. Why do you ask?"

"Simply that she was found clutching it, in a bed of
lilies. She'd been dragged into a greenhouse full of them
after she was attacked."

He was staring at her as though she was a bit cracked,
and was clearly devastated to hear such details, so she
abandoned this line of discussion and got back to more
concrete matters.

"Tell me about her, then. You were lovers, I gather?"

He had started off the interview calmly, if morosely,
and had degenerated from the moment she had butted in.
About four minutes into the questioning and he was
showing every imaginable symptom of distress. He
glanced down and mangled his huge hands together for

a while before muttering that, yes they were. Or had been, rather. He didn't know.

"Surely you know something like that?"

"Well, I suppose we were. We were very much in love, but going through a hard patch, if you see what I mean. She was a wonderful woman." The statement, being so completely at variance with the universal opinion of all the others, was quite unexpected.

"Tell me more."

"Oh, I know what the others think—hard, ruthless, ambitious. Not at all. That was just her presentation. She was very sensitive, you know. Very good-hearted; not the sort of person who would ever do something mean to anyone."

Now, there's a man in love, she thought.

"Mind you, she was slightly nervous and harried in the last few days. She was working furiously hard and it swamped everything. She was always a bit obsessed with work. It was her only doubtful quality."

"She didn't have time for you?"

"That's about it. She said it was only temporary, that she was working on something of immense importance and had to get it done. I did try to understand, but we only saw each other once a year and I was upset that she seemed to prefer the library to me. And I admit I was worried. She'd dropped people before. I wondered whether . . . Well, I was a bit jealous and resentful and began to wonder whether Miller had been right about her."

He smiled apologetically as though ashamed of the thought, and the movement transformed his bizarre face in an astonishing way. From being appallingly ugly he suddenly became quite remarkably appealing, and the sudden change caught Flavia, for a moment, quite by surprise. But it was a fleeting change; the expression lasted only an instant before the sadness and worry returned. But she saw, briefly, the attraction.

"She was a strange woman, in many ways. Forbidding, but really something very special. It annoyed me the way some of my colleagues treated her as if she wasn't there. It upset her too. I told her just to ignore them, like I did. She reckoned it wasn't that simple.

"Anyway, she worked harder, produced more, was more professional in every sense. Generous and conscientious. A small example: she was asked to write a reference for Miller's tenure, and she was going to give him a rave review. She didn't like him, didn't owe him anything, didn't like his work, but felt it would be grossly unfair if he got chucked out. Quite a lot of people would have written the man a stinker. He's really boring. And, on top of that, she loved the job. Really loved it. She hated the bickering and simply didn't notice it most of the time."

"You make her sound like Dr Kollmar."

He nodded vigorously. "Yes. Maybe that was the trouble. For some reason they didn't like each other. That painting was merely an excuse for a fight. Kollmar treated her like an amateur whose opinion he didn't respect. Which was very bad manners. He's a bit anti-American. Louise bristled and I gather said some most unfortunate things about him in return. Very unlike her."

"Such as?"

"I don't know. I didn't hear them, but Roberts was very upset. I think he was rather hoping to set a loftier tone when Bralle retired. More harmony—with him in control, of course. He's constantly going on about the dignity of the profession. Bit pompous, a touch self-important, but perhaps he means it."

He waved his hand as if to wipe away the memory of something he considered to be distasteful. "It was all pretty silly stuff," he went on apologetically, "but, despite Roberts' efforts, fairly typical of the sort of adolescent squabble that blows up every now and then. I'm sure it would have blown over eventually. For the time being, however, Kollmar got the idea she was conspiring against him and took offense. He was quite vicious about her, which was something of a shock. He's not someone you can imagine ever having strong feelings about anything except archives. About those he gets rather passionate."

"What did she do in the days after she arrived here?"

"We both arrived in Venice on Monday. For most of the time she was in the library. Thursday evening we spent together, about the first time we were alone, apart from the night we got here when I went over to her room. At the start all went well. Then she settled down to do lots of work and I didn't see much of her. She did say she would come round here on Friday night about eleven and make up to me for her distraction, but I had arranged to go out to some friends so we decided to make it another evening. Then I heard she was dead."

Flavia sympathised greatly, but knew quite well that the last thing she should do was show it. She was here to get information, not reassure and console. So, against all her natural instincts, she switched the topic of conversation, hoping to get him on to something less distressing where he would be able to give her the hints she needed.

"What was she working on?"

"No idea. I assumed it was to do with that infernal picture that she and Kollmar disagreed about, but her argument and conclusions she was keeping to herself. Apparently her paper needed last-minute rewriting. All

she said was it was awfully exciting and she would much
rather spend her time researching—she suggested a book
on someone like Giorgione—than arguing on intermi-
nable committees where no one wanted her. The idea of
quitting and flouncing off to sulk in her tent makes her
sound a bit self-pitying, but she was oddly cheerful.''

''Were you surprised by this?''

''Of course. Giorgione was her favourite painter, but
there are dozens of books on him already. On the other
hand,'' he continued, looking wistfully out of the window, ''Louise was always a bit of a romantic,''—another
novel viewpoint, she thought—''and Giorgione was the
sort of painter who would have appealed to her. You
know, the greatest painter the world has ever seen, dying
heartbroken with Titian at his bedside.''

''I thought they'd fallen out?'' she said, remembering
Roberts' conversation and wanting to appear on top of
things.

''Oh, no. Not according to Louise, anyway. Titian and
his mistress were just good friends, she reckoned. The
man who stole her from Giorgione was another painter
called Pietro Luzzi.''

''And what about her leaving the committee?'' she interrupted hurriedly.

''Oh, that. I didn't take it seriously. Everybody is always running around threatening to resign, especially
when they've just lost one of our perennial little battles.
I hadn't heard her talk like that before, but I was rather
encouraged. So was Roberts, in fact. He had been rather
concerned about her absence. He laughed and said he was
glad to hear she was beginning to settle in. You know,
starting to moan and complain like all the rest of us.''

CHAPTER

6

By the time Flavia got back to the hotel, Argyll, who had spent most of the day doing nothing constructive at all apart from wandering around churches looking at pictures, was waiting in her room. He seemed willing enough to hang about, as long as he had free use of her phone while she was in the bath. It was the moment of truth. He had finally screwed up sufficient courage to ring the Marchesa.

So she scrubbed and he dialled, and by the time Flavia had finished, pink, shiny and feeling very much more at peace with the world, both of them were in a better mood.

Argyll had revised his opinion about his ability as an art dealer. Maybe he was pretty good at it after all. Decisive, direct, fair. A good bargainer. Steely, like a poker player, he concluded.

''Bingo,'' he announced complacently when Flavia emerged in a haze of steam. ''Got her. Cut out the middleman, that's what I always say. I refused to smuggle it out once more and she said Pianta was a silly ninny—her words—for even suggesting the idea. Of course the deal was going ahead, financial details all sorted out. Victory Is Mine,'' he said with full capital letters to show how pleased he was with himself.

"My price is perfectly acceptable and she wants me to sign the contract tomorrow. So I can start arranging export permits.''

"Wonderful,'' Flavia said, genuinely pleased not only that he had at last had some success but that she wouldn't have to listen to his complaints all evening. ''We can celebrate and work on my expense account at the same time. It's been alarmingly modest all day. Then I can amuse you with all the details of my interviews this afternoon. You said you wanted to hear them.''

She had to confess—to herself, if not to Argyll whose faith in her memory she did not want to shake—that she had entirely forgotten to ask probing questions about his picture. Not, it seemed, that Masterson was ever very communicative with her colleagues anyway.

Argyll stared happily at the view of the lagoon while she disappeared back into the bathroom and dressed, then he followed as she led him to an unusually expensive restaurant, ordered a hefty aperitif and got him to down most of it before she gave him a succinct and accurate account of her day's activities.

"So there you are,'' she concluded. ''What do you think?''

"Most interesting,'' Argyll said. ''Nothing like examining the dynamics of a small group. You don't seem to have taken to Roberts all that much, I note.''

Flavia sniffed. ''Pompous pedant. All that 'We Connoisseurs' tosh.''

"Oh,'' Argyll said knowingly. ''I see. Leave the Fine Arts to us and you women stick to your knitting. That's why you've gone off him.''

"Partly. Damn it all, someone has been murdered, and apart from Van Heteren, the people I've spoken to so far don't seem very upset about it. Miller says she was ambitious and is worried mainly about the effect on his career. Roberts oozes charm all over me while saying that she might have become useful. Kollmar, it seems, thinks of her as vicious."

"She does seem very adept at antagonising people," Argyll ventured cautiously, vaguely aware that it might not be quite the right thing to say.

"You see," Flavia said indignantly, exploding with annoyance, "you're exactly the same. She gets characterised as pushy, aggressive and ambitious. Apart from Van Heteren, the best they can say of her is that she was conscientious. Conscientious! Ha! If it was Roberts, they would say how dynamic, productive and innovative he was. She produces books, articles, works like fury and Miller says she was only a token. She criticises Kollmar for shoddiness and he says she's vicious. The poor woman gets murdered and you say she antagonised people. You'll say she had it coming next. All her fault. Justifiable homicide."

Argyll looked at her in a pained fashion. There was a long silence after her outburst as she glared furiously at him.

"Are you sure you're not overidentifying a little here?" he asked.

"Of course I am. Why not? Can you imagine what it is like to work with older men who all treat you like some glorified typist? Roberts lectures me like a first year undergraduate, I'm dispatched here by Bottando on the grounds that I'm entirely innocuous, Bovolo makes slimy comments about the way I dress and only allows me to see these people because he's sure I won't accomplish anything. How would you like it?"

There was a long pause as Flavia fumed silently and Argyll felt increasingly uncomfortable. This was an aspect of her he'd not noticed before. Previously he'd always assumed that she bounced along, completely impervious to the outside world. Evidently he'd not been paying attention.

"You're quite right, of course. Sorry," he said eventually. There was another extensive lull in the conversation as Flavia depressurised and Argyll hoped his comment hadn't wrecked a perfectly good friendship. But he was again amazed how Flavia could go thermonuclear so effectively and then cool off at such speed.

"I didn't know Bottando annoyed you so much," he added when he judged the radiation level had reached safety.

Flavia looked puzzled. "Bottando? He doesn't annoy me. He does as best he can. Besides, I'm used to him now. It's everybody else. All I was saying was that you shouldn't take these accounts of Masterson at face value. Especially as one of them, possibly, is a pack of lies concocted by a murderer."

"But as far as I can see, you've made out a good case for Masterson stabbing one of these people, but have no idea why someone might have killed her," he pointed out.

"True enough."

"Back to the Sicilian marauder, then? Nice and easy, solves all the problems."

Flavia regarded him with distaste. The horrible thought that Bovolo might be right after all had crossed her mind as she came home from Van Heteren. But she dismissed the notion as being solely the result of exhaustion. She did not want the little seed of doubt cultivated by people like Argyll.

But she had no alternative theory, so they dropped the subject entirely, finished dinner and walked back to the hotel where Argyll began a lengthy speech wishing her a safe trip back to Rome. She was in two minds. On the one hand she wanted to wash her hands of this affair. It seemed like a non-starter that would lead nowhere at all and cause her a great deal of trouble *en route*. On the other, she did dislike having to leave things undone, and she knew Bovolo was going to make a total hash of it. Besides, going back to Rome to watch the possible dismemberment of the department did not fill her with enthusiasm. If she was able to come up with the real murderer, now . . .

"Oh, there's a message for you, Signorina," said the concierge as she collected her key. It was from Bovolo. Undoubtedly unimportant and could wait until morning. But adding a possibly lengthy conversation with him on to the need to see Lorenzo and Kollmar before a plane at noon made a ferociously busy morning, and she hated missing planes. Equally, it was now past ten and she felt like impressing the dour policeman with her enthusiasm. With a bit of luck she might even wake him up.

She dialled, and to her surprise was put through immediately. There followed a long series of "ums," and "ahs", and "ahas" and then silence as she listened. She turned round to summon Argyll, who was shuffling his way to the door. She gestured at him to stay put.

Eventually she mouthed her last "uh-um" and put down the phone. She turned to Argyll with a "haven't-I-got-something-to-tell-you" expression on her face.

"Well," he said. "What is it?"

"Bovolo's assistant," she said, "with the latest in-

stalment. I think my departure from Venice may have to
be delayed.''

She went back to the desk to extend her tenure of the
room.

''It appears,'' she went on, once her bed had been
secured, ''that Professor Roberts has just been fished out
of the canal, dead as they come. Come and hold my hand.
I hate stiffs.''

It was the usual sight, made unusual by the surroundings;
a thin street with two tiny walkways on either side of a
narrow and gloomy canal. A fine perspective view of
hump-backed bridges could just be made out, presenting
a picture that would, in better light and more normal circumstances, make a perfect postcard view of tourist Venice.

A few hundred yards down the canal, which runs south
from the Ca' Rezzonico on the Grand Canal, is a tiny
square, whose main claim to fame is that it contains the
small but austerely handsome church of San Barnaba. It
was almost completely dark, save for a small island of
brilliance provided by the powerful police floodlights
brought in on a patrol launch. They focused on a shape-
less bundle lying on the quayside covered by a large
white sheet.

When at last they managed to find the square, Flavia,
discreetly followed by Argyll, hurried to join a small
group of perhaps half a dozen people standing in the pool
of light. It had taken some time to get there, the topog-
raphy of Venice being especially confusing at night. But
at least it wasn't raining. During the day it had turned
very chilly and windy for the time of year and the down-
pour would undoubtedly begin soon. But not yet.

Flavia huddled inside her fur coat. She didn't particularly like it, but it was a cast-off from her mother who was under the impression that fur makes a woman more marriageable. She was constantly handing over such useful aids to matrimony, with a conscious attempt to seem less distressed about the dreadful fate of having a thirty-year-old unmarried daughter. But, whatever the potentially magical effect on eligible bachelors, the coat did not seem to stimulate the affections of Commissario Bovolo, who looked her over with great disapproval.

"We were waiting," he said flatly to Flavia, with the hidden implication that she would be better at her job if she spent less time dressing up.

"What happened?" she asked.

He shrugged. "Drowned. Don't ask me how. No way of telling. Probably slipped."

"No signs of violence?"

"Not of deliberate violence, if that's what you mean." He knew very well that it was.

"How long's he been dead?"

Bovolo shrugged again. "Can't say really. Not long. He was found about an hour and a half ago by the refuse collectors. They dropped a sack overboard, fished for it and found him instead. Spent twenty minutes in their boat while they waited for us. He pongs a bit, I'm afraid," he concluded.

An unnecessary detail, but more than accurate. They wandered over to the side of the canal where a small group of miscellaneous officials was gathered. At the focal point of their gaze was one of the world's greatest experts on Renaissance painting, not that the casual passer-by would have realised.

Professor Roberts' appearance was not improved by his hand-spun Harris tweed jacket being covered liberally with potato peelings and his scholarly authority was di-

minished by the very strong odour that now emanated
from him. The once elegantly coiffed mane of grey-white
hair was wet and grimy and tangled up with lumps of . . .

Flavia screwed up her face in disgust and switched
quickly to thinking about something other than the inadequate state of the Venetian sewage system. She hadn't
taken to the man enormously, but was inclined to think
he deserved a more seemly end than this.

"Is that all you can say? He was found at about nine-
thirty?" Bovolo nodded. "When did he drop in,
though?"

"As far as we can guess at the moment, probably
seven, or thereabouts. We might know more when the
doctors have poked him about a bit."

He called over one of his subordinates who was throwing pieces of wood into the water and watching them
intensely. Flavia had assumed he was underemployed,
but was soon disabused of this notion. "Well?" he asked
as the man came over.

The pimply youth stood to attention and spoke in the
strange accent of the born and bred Venetian. "About
two hundred metres an hour, as far as I can see, sir. The
current brings the water down from the Grand Canal."

Bovolo turned smugly to Flavia. "Venetian lore.
That's why we aren't too keen on strangers butting in,"
he said, a little unreasonably considering that his own
accent marked him clearly as a Milanese. "What it means
is that this"—he gestured at Roberts' mortal remains—
"must have fallen in between about four and six hundred
metres upstream, depending on when he entered the water."

The young policeman began to talk again, but Bovolo
shut him up impatiently. He was enjoying himself. He
pointed towards the Grand Canal. "Probably went in at

the Ca' Rezzonico vaporetto stop. Must have walked there from his house further down this little canal here. We'll have to go and check for signs of a slip. Interview all the inhabitants, that sort of thing. Nasty accident. Very nasty."

"You think this was an accident?" Argyll said incredulously, speaking for the first time. Bovolo glared at him coldly and Flavia trod heavily on his foot. He shut up while Flavia negotiated to get copies of the postmortem and investigations out of the local man. Bovolo, glancing suspiciously at Argyll from time to time, eventually agreed.

"Don't get any fancy ideas, mind," he said by way of a farewell. "Remember your role here. And please don't think this little incident need delay your departure. I'm sure you're needed more in Rome than you are here."

His voice faded as Flavia strode off out of the square, with Argyll in hot pursuit.

"No need to run," he called as she rounded the corner out of sight of the watching Bovolo. "You're not in a race."

She slowed down when they were out of earshot, and carefully chose a quiet and secluded little alleyway. She went down it, screamed loudly for a few seconds to let out forty-eight hours' worth of pent up frustration, and kicked the wall with her boots.

Argyll, hands in pockets, waited patiently for her to finish. She was prone to high-decibel ventilation every now and then. Her language was diabolical.

"Better?" he asked calmly when she quietened down a bit.

"Damn that stupid, moronic, complacent little . . . person," she screeched with bitterness as she tried to digest both Bovolo's remarks and conclusions.

"You think he might be wrong?"

"Wrong?" Argyll winced as a light in a nearby house clicked on and an inquiring head poked out to discover what all the noise was about. "Ha. How can anyone be that dimwitted? Nasty accident. Paf!"

"Well, I thought it was hasty of him," Argyll said, trying to get her to express herself a little more quietly. "So why did you stand on my foot then? You're always doing that. It hurts, you know."

He persuaded her to leave the alleyway, and they crossed a narrow bridge with Flavia calmer but still percolating nicely. Twice in an evening. Quite a lot of energy used up, even for her. She picked up a stone lying on the concrete parapet and hurled it into the canal below to vent a bit more of her supply and was rewarded with a bellow of outrage from the owner of the barge just passing underneath.

"Oh, shut up," she yelled back. "I didn't hit you. And you can shut up as well," she said furiously, swinging round to Argyll who was convulsed with laughter.

Argyll gurgled away and tried to control his voice so that he could speak coherently. "I am sorry," he began, before being interrupted by another burst of laughter. Quite unconsciously and not thinking as he giggled again, he put his arm round her and gave her a comradely hug.

"Don't be absurd," she said tartly, so full of irritation that the leftovers spilled on to her companion as well. Argyll stopped laughing and withdrew his arm.

"Sorry," he said soberly. "It's serious, I know."

"That's right," she said stiffly but beginning to realise

she was overreacting. "God, but I feel tired all of a sudden."

"Want a walk? Clear the brain? You sound as though a brisk canter through the streets would do you good."

She shook her head. "No. The evening's been going from bad to worse. The longer it lasts the worse it will get. I want to go back to the hotel and go straight to bed. I'm exhausted."

CHAPTER

7

She was sitting apathetically at the breakfast table when Argyll arrived once more. She waved him over and he plonked himself down heavily opposite. The dynamic art dealer of the night before was a little under the weather this morning.

"How are you?" he asked flatly. "You look a bit peaky."

She grunted. "OK, I suppose. You don't seem so great either. What's up?"

Argyll eyed the breakfast with distaste. "Well, maybe nothing," he said reluctantly. "But I was due to go round to the Marchesa's today to make the arrangements for picking up the pictures. Remember? So I rang up, just to say when I would arrive, and got a very frosty reception. I spoke to Pianta again, who seems to be trying to interpose her body, as it were. She said I was not to come. Can't think why."

"Maybe they're going shopping or something. Doesn't really matter, does it? I mean, the Marchesa has agreed to sell."

"I hope so. But I haven't got the contract yet. It just makes me a little uneasy. Instinct. You're not eating much, I note. Always a bad sign."

She poked a croissant miserably. "That's because I'm not doing very well up here. I was sent to help clear up one death. And, blow me, now there're two of them. And I can't help feeling that it's my fault."

"Why?"

"Obvious, isn't it? Something in the way I questioned them set things off. Then, splat."

"Well, I don't know. It doesn't sound as though any of them were unduly disturbed. You hardly approached them as though you were eyeing them up for a prison cell. But I must admit that to the outside world a second murder won't be instantly applauded as rapid progress."

Flavia grunted once more. She could see that without his pointing it out. "You reckon it was a murder, then, despite Bovolo? Have you had breakfast?"

"Yes and no. And yes. That is, I think it was murder, I haven't had breakfast and, in answer to your unspoken question, I would love some. My appetite increases when I'm worried."

She ordered for him and, after a moment's consideration, decided to abstain herself. Argyll looked at her with concern.

"I suppose," he said after a brief pause, "that he *could* have tripped. But you must admit it seems a bit unlikely."

One thing about Argyll—idiot though he often was—he did tend to take her point of view. She was about to answer when the waiter, that angel of mercy, that deliverer of good tidings, returned in a soft glide of polished shoes and glinting chromium. She studied the pile of fresh rolls and croissants and jam piled up in front of Argyll, and began to feel a mite peckish.

"Perhaps. But it doesn't sound as though Bovolo will agree," she said, reaching for a roll and covering it daintily with jam. Force yourself to eat something, she thought. Stop brooding.

"An accident would, of course, be a simple solution."

"Nonsense," she replied brusquely, wiping her lips and eyeing a croissant.

"So you keep on hunting."

"Can't do that. The report goes to the local investigating magistrate's office. If he decides the case is closed, that's that."

"Except, of course, that it may be wrong."

"Apart from that little detail, yes. Why do you think it was murder?" she asked, spearing a few cubes of melon.

"Too much coincidence, that's all. It seems more reasonable to assume that someone popped him one. You've eaten all of my breakfast, did you know that?" he ended with a disappointed tone in his voice.

She had no chance to defend herself. She was about to recommend ordering some more when she noticed a large and portly figure heading towards them from the dining-room entrance.

"Good God," she said.

"Ah. I thought I might find you in the dining room," said Bottando with an air of complacent satisfaction on his face as he approached. "Just a hunch, you know."

"What on earth are you doing here?"

He looked at her curiously. "Work, of course. What else would bring me to this awful place? I did try to ring, but you've always been a sound sleeper. Some more pictures have gone missing. Thought I'd come and have a poke around, and see how you were getting on. I hope you appreciate my presence as fully as you should. I've just suffered a whole miserable hour on one of those flying tin cans to get here and I feel very fragile. I gather,'' he added, glancing at the breakfast plates, ''that there's been another death.''

He paused, ordered some breakfast and added an extra order for Flavia to be sure of getting some himself.

''Mr Argyll. What a surprise.'' He made it sound as though it was nothing of the sort. Argyll suddenly had the feeling that the General was deducing things from their joint breakfast.

''We were discussing this case,'' he explained, trying to set the record straight as quickly as possible. ''I seem to have got involved in it a little.''

Bottando shut his eyes and groaned quietly. ''Oh, dear,'' he said. ''And I was rather hoping this would be a day trip.''

''Jonathan's been extremely helpful,'' Flavia explained. She knew that Bottando had always considered Argyll to be a little accident-prone, the sort of person who could make simple things elaborately complicated. Admittedly, he had some reason for thinking this. But justice demanded she explain matters properly.

''I'm sure he has,'' Bottando said grumpily. ''The trouble is, that it's largely because of him that I'm here.''

Argyll just beat Flavia to raising his eyebrows in surprise. He did it faster; but she was able to raise them one at a time, an accomplishment he'd always envied. ''I don't like the sound of that,'' he observed.

''I'm not surprised. Last night, at about eleven, a dozen or so pictures were pinched from a palazzo in Venice. Nothing exciting about that. Happens all the time. But as the owner said she thought the most likely person to have pinched them was Jonathan Argyll, I thought that—''

"What!" Argyll squeaked in horror. "Me? Why would anyone say that I—''

"The pictures were—or are, I suppose, if you want to be technical—owned by the Marchesa di Mulino. It seems you were negotiating to buy them. You didn't like the price being asked, so went ahead and obtained them much more cheaply. So she reckons. Or rather the person who lodged the complaint does, a Signora Pianta.''

Argyll was getting considerable practice at rocking backwards and forwards on his chair. He did it again now, opened his mouth several times with no sound coming out and wiped his hand over his forehead in what appeared to be a gesture of concern. Bottando, who had encountered the Englishman's occasional moments of incoherence before, was not tempted to interpret the display as necessarily a sign of guilt.

"Of course," he said, filling in the empty space until Argyll should recover himself enough to regain his speech, "it seems a little unlikely. But, what with one thing and another, I thought it best to take on the investigation myself.'' He smiled encouragingly. "I hope you appreciate this. I left the budget submissions behind at a very delicate stage.''

"They're gone?" Argyll said, callously ignoring Bottando's administrative problems. "How? It's ridiculous. I'd agreed to buy them already. I was going round this morning to sign the contract. This is terrible,'' he babbled.

Bottando spread his stubby hands on the table. "I'm merely repeating the story as it came to me very early this morning. Very early, I repeat. Not that I expect thanks. I don't suppose you have an alibi for the time in question, do you?''

"Of course. I was with Flavia.''

Bottando, something of a romantic at heart, beamed at him in a way which indicated he had misunderstood the situation entirely. "Excellent. But I suppose that means you didn't steal them.''

"Of course not,'' Argyll said indignantly.

"What a shame. Think how much easier it would be for me. You wouldn't like to make a tiny little confession, just to make an old man's declining years that bit easier, I suppose?''

"No. I didn't pinch the damn things. I wouldn't know how to begin. Besides, where do you think I put them? In my hotel room? What was stolen anyway?''

Bottando produced a list and handed it over. "I knew you weren't going to be helpful, somehow,'' he commented wistfully.

Argyll read and Flavia craned over to see. "All my pictures,'' he said miserably.

"Including the Masterson portrait,'' Flavia added. Bottando asked her to explain.

"Louise Masterson was interested in one of these very unimportant pictures Jonathan was negotiating to buy. At the moment we don't know why.''

"I knew it,'' her boss said heavily. "I think I shall get this friend of yours deported. Go on then. Tell me all.''

Bottando had almost finished eating by the time she stopped. True to his word, he had kept absolutely silent, apart from the odd grunt and nod as she spoke. He was a good listener, and always respectful. It was one of his better qualities. His mood also seemed to improve notably as he recovered from the epic of the morning flight from Rome. Flavia could never understand how someone like him could get into such a tizz over aircraft.

"You see, I was right," he said benevolently when she finished. "The moment Mr Argyll here gets involved things become tortuous and thoroughly difficult. When I sent you up here it was a simple mugging. Now look at it. A complete mess." There was, however, a hint of a twinkle in his eye as he spoke. It seemed to refresh him that such an apparently dull affair might have something in it to justify his coming all this way after all. "What are your opinions?"

He addressed both of them, implicitly signalling to Argyll that his presence was forgiven and he could feel free to speak. Still, the latter, feeling a little bruised by the traumas of the morning, thought it better to keep a low profile.

"I haven't interviewed everyone yet," she began. "But if we assume Masterson was killed by someone who knew her, rather than by a mythical Sicilian, then there are five likely candidates—the other people on the committee. If you knock out Roberts—as someone else already has, so to speak—then we're down to four."

"So," interrupted Bottando, "perhaps it would be best just to wait another forty-eight hours and narrow the field down a bit more?"

"Ho, ho. As I was saying, all have decent alibis, so there is no way at the moment of eliminating them that way. Firstly, there is Miller. He was condescending about her. Implied she was all flash and ambition; not a real scholar at all. Certain amount of jealousy there; she was much more successful. On the other hand, no real motive and needed her for a reference. Equally, seems to have been Roberts' little poodle."

Bottando nodded. "Not very convincing," he said happily. "Try again."

"Secondly, there is Kollmar. I'm seeing him this morning but it is common knowledge he and Masterson had a spat about a picture he'd examined. The two did not get on, although he and Roberts were long-time colleagues. Also seems a bit under Roberts' thumb. The point is, Roberts wanted Kollmar to deliver some papers to him yesterday evening, and the body was found floating down the canal near where he lived. Alibi for Masterson good."

"Still not convincing, but worth looking into," Bottando observed.

"Thirdly, Roberts. No motive at all for doing in Masterson, as far as I could see. And, of course, he is dead himself. He was a precious little toad but was Masterson's patron."

Bottando nodded.

"Finally, leaving aside Lorenzo whom I also haven't seen yet, there is Van Heteren, whose affair with Masterson may have blown a fuse. Bit of jealousy, perhaps. An impetuous man, I guess, possible candidate for a Crime of Passion, but the sort of person—I would have thought—who would be overcome with remorse and confess immediately afterwards. Besides, another good alibi and no reason that I can see for rubbing out Roberts."

"What was she doing in that garden?"

"Don't know. Bovolo reckons she was waiting for a taxi to get back to the island because of the transport strike, but it's still a mystery. The theft of these pictures is a new one, assuming that there's a connection."

"Why should there be?"

"Search me. But when a woman is interested in an obscure picture, she gets murdered and the picture is stolen a few days later, then I begin to get a little itch."

Bottando poured himself another coffee, added a minuscule amount of milk and a vast quantity of sugar, and stirred meditatively.

"It's very thin," he said carefully, not wishing to cause offence. "I know you've only been at it for a day or so, but there's nothing solid here at all."

She nodded sadly. "I know. But Bovolo is such a pain it's amazing I've got that far. I'll spend the day talking to them again. I also thought that maybe Jonathan here could go through all the papers and committee minutes and so on that Bovolo gave me. The carabinieri didn't notice anything of interest, but you never know. That is, I thought it would be a good idea until you turned up and—"

"And suggested I might be involved as well," Argyll added. "Touchy. Maybe I ought to bow out here and go back to Rome. Otherwise I might end up being accused of murder as well. Besides which, I don't want to damage the department. Wouldn't look good, you using a suspected felon as an unofficial assistant."

"Good heavens, young man, no. I'm sure there's no need for that. I've no doubt your alibi is delightful for both murders. And, if you had nothing to do with those, then there is no reason to think you had anything to do with the theft," he said, although he did not succeed in reassuring the Englishman overmuch.

"Anyway, this theft is under my authority, not that of the carabinieri. So I can authorise you to do as Flavia suggests. As long as my authority lasts, which may not be very long, the way things are going."

"Still the budgets?"

"Afraid so. Getting very sticky. It's not quite reached the stage of colleagues asking me what I shall do during my retirement, but it's getting close. Oh, well," he went on, folding up his napkin with care. "Nothing to be done about that at the moment. Mr Argyll, you spend the morning reading. Flavia, you will have to stay on and go about your interviews, and I will trot off and see what I can do with your friend Commissario Bovolo. What's he like, by the way?"

"Not your sort," she told him. "Cold, unwelcoming and as thick as two short planks. You won't get on, especially if you threaten to complicate a case he wants to gift wrap and hand over to the investigating magistrate as soon as possible. Besides, he views the impending end of the department with peculiar glee, although why it concerns him I don't know. See you later." She got up, checked her bag, and marched off.

While Bottando and Flavia were dealing with the living and the only recently deceased, Argyll spent the morning engrossed in the study of the long-since dead. To wit, he went to the Biblioteca Marciana, the long and delightful hall of learning that occupies a good part of the southern side of the Piazza San Marco. His plan was simple and he was rather proud of it.

For a start, he was going to spend a few hours not worrying about the business of buying pictures, earning a living and other distressing things. He'd considered rushing straight round to the Marchesa and making sure he could, at least, acquire the few paintings that remained. But as he reckoned it might be better to let the General reassure everyone about his innocence first, he decided to wait until everybody calmed down.

He was meant to go through the committee's business papers and so glanced through them fast without noticing anything of interest. Mainly a record of paintings examined, reports written, votes taken. He scribbled a few notes for the purpose of looking conscientious, then turned to other, more interesting questions.

He had planned to use his charm and persuasive powers to get the librarian to hand over the slips of paper Masterson would have used to order up her books. The task was much easier than he'd anticipated. He'd just launched into his explanation about Masterson to the somewhat forbidding lady in charge of the desk, when she leant over to poke around in a box on the floor and pulled out a large envelope.

If the American was dead, she asked irritably, who was going to pay for these? These, it turned out, being a pile of photocopies Masterson had ordered the evening she was killed. She managed to convey the impression that it was the height of discourtesy to get yourself murdered before paying your bills.

Argyll's volunteering to take the packet off her hands cheered her up immensely, however, and, once he had gone over to the cash desk and handed out what seemed to him an outrageous sum in payment, he went back, took delivery, and settled down to read what she'd been up to.

Whatever her personal spikiness, Masterson was no slow-coach, that was clear. In a single evening, she appeared to have ploughed her way through more than a dozen books. Argyll, who could rarely get through a chapter in a library without falling sound asleep, was duly impressed. Such industry always made him feel inferior. Suppressing a sigh, he steeled himself for the arduous task of dogging her literary footsteps wherever they might lead.

Which was, as far as he could tell after the first hour, not very far. She seemed to have already adopted her resolution to forget about the committee and concentrate on Giorgione. There was Vasari's and Ridolfi's *Lives of the Painters*, both in rather handsome seventeenth-century editions. Leather covers, nice gold tooling on the spine, that sort of thing. As far as Giorgione was concerned, the only fact they seemed to agree on was that his mistress was called Violante di Modena. With proper Renaissance morality, they noted she dropped dead soon after leaving him, although they disagreed about whose arms she was in at the time. Still, both reckoned that it served her right for two-timing a genius, and were upset that Giorgione had seen fit to die of a broken heart as a result.

Next a brief biography of Pietro Luzzi, the pupil of Giorgione tipped as the more likely candidate for the post of red-hot lover who'd seduced and run off with Violante. Evidence seemed a bit thin here. Apart from the fact that he was killed in a battle in 1511, the writer seemed to know nothing about him. Nor, indeed, did he seem to care, hinting rather strongly that painters of Luzzi's limited ability and dubious character were best forgotten.

The references to Titian were incidental, and unfortunately were strikingly lacking in any proof that he had painted the Marchesa's portrait or, indeed, was connected with it in any way. There were extracts from old accounts of how he had gone to Padua to paint scenes from the life of the town's patron saint. A book of Venice city records containing a petition from Alfonso di Modena— that surname again, Argyll thought—requesting that the artist be allowed to return because of the great services he had performed. This with a footnote that the authorities disliked artisans leaving town without permission, as Titian evidently had when he rushed off to Padua. Descriptions of the three Padua pictures themselves wrapped the reading up.

All very edifying, no doubt, but not what you might call full of significant hints that would lead inevitably to the door of a murderer.

He was beginning to get frustrated with all this nonsense. So, being a practical soul, he funnelled the photocopies back into the envelope, returned the books, then headed off to the nearest affordable café—he was too wise to be caught out going into one of the ferociously expensive places in the Piazza San Marco—and ordered a drink.

Flavia had arranged the night before with Franz Kollmar to meet at the house he was renting on the Giudecca, the long strip of a rather unfashionable island that runs along the south of Venice proper. On the boat over to the island she read the police notes to get some idea of who she was about to be meeting. It was not an impressive collection of facts. Job in Baden-Baden, specialist in sixteenth-century Italian painting, married with six children aged between one and fourteen. Six children? That seemed a little excessive. Aged forty-three, founder member of the committee, well thought of professionally.

The boat was drawing into the shore at San Eufemia. Fortunately for her already battered and humiliated sense of direction, the house that the German lived in was close to the quayside; a short walk down the rio di San Eufemia, and there was a small dwelling, beaten, neglected and sunless.

She was still breathless when she rang the bell, and was let in by an attractive but harassed woman—evidently Frau Kollmar—and shown into a small salon. Clearly, Kollmar was not a wealthy man. The house was not nearly big enough for such an evidently voluminous family, she thought as she removed a teddy bear from the sofa and sat down. It was probably not too expensive to rent either; the furniture was cheap, the paintwork peeling. All in all, it had a depressed air that not even the presence of a small army of little Kollmars did much to dispel.

In another room she could hear the high-pitched tones of a baby crying its head off. A lower pitched, man's voice could also be distinguished, shushing the infant and assuring it—in German but the language used to calm crying babies is universally comprehensible—not to worry everything was fine and just be a good girl.

Flavia sat with a doll on her knee and a patient expression on her face. Gradually the screaming faded and came to an abrupt stop with a throaty gurgle and congratulatory noises from the relieved parent. A few seconds later, the relieved parent himself appeared through the door. Kollmar was evidently a right-thinking father who tried to do his bit with the children but who found the experience a harrowing one. He did not look at all happy; movements nervous, voice abrupt, although whether that was due to anxiety over her presence or combat fatigue from battling with the feeding bottle was not immediately clear.

Certainly, she thought, the members of this committee were an ill-assorted lot. Roberts the cultured connoisseur, Masterson the dour businesswoman. And this besplattered apparition, all nerves and nappies. On appearance and personality alone it was not surprising they had disagreements.

They talked in Italian; Kollmar's diction made him sound like something out of an old war movie, but he was fearfully accurate. His main fault was that he spoke far too well ever to pass for an Italian. If you can learn German you can learn anything, but the accomplishment does seem to breed a tendency to show off with linguistic fireworks. Flavia mentally ducked to avoid the barrage of imperfect subjunctives that flew through the air whenever he opened his mouth.

"I'm sure you will excuse me if we keep this interview short," he said, somewhat to Flavia's surprise. "I have a great deal of work to do and I think I have spent more than enough time talking to the police in the last few days already."

"I would have thought that the sudden death of two of your colleagues would merit some of your time," she replied sharply. That's telling him, she thought.

Kollmar's look of consternation was, at least, convincing. He paused, looked at her as though she was a little mad, frowned and shifted in his seat in the manner of someone who knows something fishy is going on.

"Two?" he said eventually, latching on to the important bit. "What are you talking about?"

"You haven't been told?"

Kollmar's bewilderment was impressive, and the way his face crumpled in horror when she told him about Roberts' death even more so. She made it as gory as possible. Not because she was hard-hearted, although she hadn't taken much of a liking to the man, just that she reckoned people watch their words less carefully if in a state of shock. She was inclined, on the basis of his horrified reaction alone, to lower the odds on his being responsible for the Englishman's end. She noted that he did not appear nearly so upset about Masterson.

"Dead?" he asked, a little stupidly. "I don't believe it. But why wasn't I told? Good heavens, I am now the senior person on the committee. Surely I have a right to be informed of such matters?''

Flavia just managed to restrain her expression of surprise at such a bizarre statement. To stand on your dignity at such a moment struck her as being petty, if not downright callous. She imagined he hadn't been informed probably because the police were being characteristically inefficient and just hadn't got around to it. On the other hand, she thought, remembering Bralle's nickname for the man, Kollmar was exactly the sort of person who you would forget to inform. Best to pass over the comment in silence.

''You delivered some papers to Professor Roberts' house last night, I believe,'' she said. ''What time was that?''

''About eight,'' he replied. ''On my way home for dinner. He wasn't in, so I just pushed them through the door with a note. Why?''

''That was about the time he was killed.''

''Oh, dear God,'' he said, considering the implications and not liking them. ''And you think I . . . ?''

''Not necessarily. But I don't know of anyone else in the area at the time. Were you alone?''

He nodded with an increasingly dismayed look on his face, the appearance of someone who has woken up from a bad dream and finds that it is all coming true.

''But this is ridiculous,'' he resumed after shaking his head in disbelief for a bit. ''I do not believe this tragedy could possibly be murder. I cannot accept that anyone would want to kill Roberts. Not an enemy in the world. Such a dynamic, productive and innovative man.''

Flavia snorted. ''And Masterson?'' she asked.

''Entirely diff . . .'' he began, then stopped.

"Different? You mean she did have enemies? Like yourself, perhaps?"

"That is also ridiculous," he said primly, beginning to fight back a little. "We had professional disagreements. Nothing more. I can't say I liked the woman. In fact I found her most difficult. But if people went round assassinating all difficult colleagues, there'd be no one left."

Point taken. Flavia herself could have supplied several hundred good candidates. "All right, then. Suppose you tell me why she was difficult?"

He considered this carefully. "How can I explain it?" he began. "As I'm sure you know, the study of art is a very special discipline. With an enterprise like our committee, there had to be common feeling and understanding between all members for it to work properly. There had to be sympathy, and a mutual approach, if you see what I mean."

He smiled in a way that suggested that he didn't really expect her to understand such fine points. Flavia leant back in her armchair, crossed her arms and tried to suppress her feelings of pique.

"For some considerable time, such a belief in our co-operative enterprise existed. Alas, of late, I'm afraid that the meetings have been more characterised by discord than the harmony which would be more appropriate and more productive."

Here he stopped, unwilling to go into further and unseemly detail. Flavia reckoned the time had come to give him a helping hand.

"You mean that the arrival of Dr Masterson disrupted your cosy little brotherhood and she was causing waves?"

That didn't go down at all well. Kollmar took on more

and more the air of an injured saint. If Louise Masterson was half as direct in her conversational style, there would have been no chance the two could have cooperated.

"That was one element. Another was the constant pressure from Dr Lorenzo for us to hurry our work. He is a man with many qualities, but I fear he is prepared to accept methods which are perhaps unduly hasty in order to impress his patrons in Rome."

"But tell me more about Louise Masterson."

"Far be it from me to criticise her, especially in the circumstances, but she was an undoubtedly forceful woman in a field which above all calls for—how can I put it?—reflection, patience and a willingness to learn."

"You mean she disagreed with you?"

"I mean she disagreed with everyone. I gather, for example, that she was writing a most unfavourable reference for Dr Miller, even though she knew it might cost him his job. I find that sort of behaviour quite unforgivable."

"What makes you think she was doing that?"

He looked defensive all of a sudden. "Um, I can't remember. I believe Roberts told me. He was unconcerned about it, on the grounds that his own reference would more than make up for it. But he was upset, no doubt about that. Quite right too.

"In my own case, she did dispute some of my conclusions about a painting owned by a collector in Milan. Initially I was inclined to let it pass, until I discovered she was waging a campaign against me behind my back."

"What do you mean?"

"I was warned by Professor Roberts that she was saying most unfortunate things about me. Poor man, he was clearly distressed. I do so hate that sort of thing. At the meeting, to my face, all she said was that she wanted to examine the picture a little herself. Next thing I find that she is calling my judgement and scholarship into question and saying the whole thing will have to be redone. I fear that she found a ready ear in Dr Lorenzo."

"But you didn't want a fight?"

"Certainly not. I was confident I was being appropriately cautious. It is an important business, attributing paintings. Better safe than sorry. I was undecided until Roberts himself concluded the thing was probably a dud."

That wasn't quite what Roberts had said, she remembered, but she let it pass. "And what conclusions had Dr Masterson come to?"

Kollmar pursed his lips and shook his head. "How should I know? I cannot say we discussed the matter. The only time we mentioned the subject I found her attitude rather offensive."

"Why?"

"This was Friday afternoon, while we were leaving after the session and attempting to get off the island. It was the last time I spoke to her. I was trying to effect some reconciliation, so I suggested a drink. She refused. I must say, I thought it was a bit rude, considering that I made the approach. I had no need to, after all. Roberts and Miller heard her. I could tell they were a bit taken aback as well.

"But that was what she was like, I'm afraid. You see," he said earnestly, "she always wanted to win. She wasn't really into the exchange of ideas; she wanted to beat anyone who disagreed with her. That I have always found insupportable. Especially in a woman."

She let that one pass as well and congratulated herself on her remarkable forbearance that morning. So you slipped out of the opera, lured her into the gardens and knifed her seven times, she thought in a speculative sort of fashion. Still didn't sound right somehow, however desirable a solution it was.

"And do you have any theories about these deaths?"

"For poor Roberts I can only assume it was a most tragic accident. As for Masterson, I understand she was robbed and then murdered in the struggle. She was a very forceful woman who would always have fought back. No robber would have taken her briefcase without having to fight for it. She was always combative. I'm sorry it turned out to be a quality that cost her her life."

"And at the time Dr Masterson was murdered you were at the theatre with your wife and Professor Roberts?"

"Indeed. It was our first night out together for months. We got a babysitter from next door and went out around eight and came back well after midnight."

"And you went by taxi?"

"Oh, yes. We had to. No choice. We were lucky. Because of the strike we nearly didn't get there at all. It took hours to get back as well. I'm afraid that took some of the pleasure out of an otherwise splendidly generous gesture on Roberts' part. He got some late returns and rang to invite us. Most kind, especially as he is no great fan of Donizetti. He even bought champagne for us to drink during the interval. As I say, a most generous man."

There then followed a long silence; Flavia had run out of things to ask and already had quite enough to think about. There seemed little point in asking more about Roberts: no enemies, no one who could possibly want to kill such a good, distinguished man, etc. His answers were obvious. So she ran through the usual parting patter about how he mustn't be disturbed, very distressing but all routine and necessary, she said with her most winning smile. He seemed scarcely reassured.

The three of them met, as arranged, in a restaurant near Santa Maria Formosa for lunch. It was one of those delightful lunches that happen only on rare occasions, when the food is perfect and all the company in a harmonious mood. Only the weather was being uncooperative, but it was at least still restraining itself in the matter of rain.

Considering that there were two murders, one theft, a threatened coup against the department and the likely displeasure of Edward Byrnes to deal with, it occurred to Argyll that the jolly mood was a little carefree, if not irresponsible. But Bottando was too much of a professional to let such matters disturb his enjoyment of a good feed and he, by virtue of his seniority and the fact that he was paying, set the tone. His good humour was even more remarkable as he had spent most of the morning in the company of Roberts and Bovolo, the one dead, the other a little pale and colourless.

"Smug, he was," he said, referring to the latter. "Reckons he'll get a good deal of praise for wrapping this one up so fast. So much so that he didn't even object when I said you'd be staying on to help me with this theft. As long as you keep your nose out of matters which are none of your business, so he said with what I gather is his normal charm.

"Anyway, his report will be finished by this evening, all squared with the investigating magistrate by tomorrow. Sicilian and Roberts' own carelessness. Apparently they're on an efficiency drive to cut costs. He kept on talking about through-put and case solution ratios. Accompanied by a subtle warning about how interference from Rome makes for inefficiency. I'm sure he couldn't have meant us. All this taking place in the mortuary in the presence of a somewhat ominous and hostile magistrate. I have, by the way, found out why Bovolo is so opposed to us.''

''Why?'' Flavia asked curiously.

''Because he will head the carabinieri's art department in Venice if it is all devolved to the provinces. Very worrying for us, but a pleasant prospect for the art thieves. I didn't realise the carabinieri had got that far in their planning. They must be more confident than I thought.

''Anyway, old Bovolo's promotion rather depends on us getting it in the neck, so he will help that process along as much as possible. That's also why he is so anxious to get this case tidied up in record time.''

''So why did you want to see him?''

''Oh, I don't know really. Thought I should; know your enemy. I was glad I did. I had a brief chat with the pathologist. His report mentions a mark on Roberts' neck.''

''Where did that come from?''

''Where indeed? The pathologist muttered something about tight collars, but it seems equally possible that someone grabbed him by the neck. I'm no expert of course, but the pathologist rather reluctantly agreed that it could be. He confessed that he wanted to lay out all the options in his report, but was told by the magistrate to make up his mind and stick to it. His contract is coming up for renewal. I advised him to play safe.''

''Why did you do that?'' Flavia asked in surprise. ''There's every reason to believe that Roberts was killed, probably by the person who killed Masterson. A murderer is going to get off . . .''

Bottando held up his hands to stop the flow of indignation. "Your conscience does you credit, my dear, but your brains are letting the side down a bit. Think. If the murder investigation is left open, Bovolo is in charge and will do his best to keep us out of it. And remember his track record. So far he's taken aim at a probably nonexistent Sicilian and is now entranced by the prospect of Roberts' drowning by accident. Disabuse him of that notion and he may well end up arresting Argyll here.

"After all, it's not my fault the man is an idiot. This way he is content and we have a free hand to do what we will. As I suspect we won't find the pictures without finding ourselves a murderer, we can now go ahead unhindered. All we have to do is make sure we get a result before next Monday."

"Why next . . . ? Oh, of course. That's when the budget goes in, isn't it?"

Bottando nodded conspiratorially.

"Is that why you came up here? To see if you could grab a bit of credit and impress the minister?"

He looked a bit sheepish. "Well," he said reluctantly, "I was also concerned that Mr Argyll shouldn't be unfairly suspected of any crime, you know. Especially because you are such good friends. That connection might not be too healthy in the wrong hands. Still," he said airily, "if we manage this one as well, I would not be loth to draw it to the attention of the appropriate authorities."

"I'm ashamed of you."

"Why? What would you do in my position? We have little time at our disposal. So, please, tell me how you've been spending it, my dear."

He was the only person in the world who could "my dear" Flavia and get away with it. It was so obviously

devoid of any lack of respect—and so much his style—
that Flavia would have been worried now if he'd stopped.
She wiped her mouth on her napkin and recited.

Lorenzo, she said, having disposed of Kollmar, was
not at all what she expected. He was evidently from an
old Venetian family and combined all the airs and graces
with a surprisingly sharp mind. He had received her in
his apartment which faced on to one of the more crumbly
parts of the rio Nuovo. The building was run-down, with
the sort of tattiness that only the very secure could manage. For all that, he was no decadent. In his mid-forties
and very suave.

"A very handsome man, I must say," she added par-
enthetically. "Fair hair, deep set, hazel eyes, finely chis-
elled features . . ."

"All right, all right," said Argyll a little impatiently.
Bottando smiled gently at him. "Get on with it."

Flavia frowned at him. "It's important," she said. "I
was trying to give you an idea of what he's like. No
matter," she continued, getting back to her narrative
flow. "He was very courteous. A bit of an entrepreneur.
Power-broker type, you know. On lots of committees,
editorial boards, advisory councils. Constantly whizzing
around, fixing things. Levered himself on to the Titian
committee by being a second cousin twice removed of
the arts minister's wife. Also happens to be the nephew
of your Marchesa. Clearly knows his stuff, but sees himself as more of an administrator. Leaves the scholarly end
to everyone else.

"For all that, I must say I rather liked him. He's awfully enthusiastic, has a good sense of humour—which
seems singularly lacking in most of the others—and was
suitably upset about all these deaths. Although in the case
of Roberts I think he was much more concerned about

the effects on the committee and his own career. Not much love lost between them, I think.''

''Do you know why he and Roberts didn't get on?'' Argyll interrupted.

''Essentially it was what the others hinted at: a good old-fashioned power struggle. This man Bralle founded the thing, and leaves when Roberts organises the state grant. Bralle didn't like the idea much but the others supported it as they were all short of cash. Roberts expects to be the kingpin, but shortly after the money arrives, along comes Lorenzo as well. They've been at loggerheads ever since.''

''Any solid reason behind it? Apart from power, that is?''

''According to Lorenzo—and there's only his word for it—he wants two things. Firstly, speedier results, because otherwise they might take the subsidy away. More importantly, he wants to go methodically, starting on pictures in Italian museums, then working out. He casts himself as a bit of a patriot. You know, defender of the national heritage.''

''That's perfectly sound, isn't it?'' said Bottando, who rather liked to see himself in a similar fashion.

''Yes. But it is not the way they were used to doing it. Previously it was more random, going after easily accessible stuff all over the place and mainly in private hands. Nothing wrong with that either. But that, ostensibly at least, is what the struggle is about. If you study pictures in Italy, you need people to work in Italy. Which the rest of the committee can't do. So you get new people, who will be buddies of Lorenzo . . .''

''Ah. I see. How's his alibi stand up?'' Bottando asked.

''Very nicely.''

"Oh. Pity."

"He was with his mistress, girlfriend, call her what you will, at the time. I spoke to her alone and she gave more than sufficiently graphic details of his every move to convince me Lorenzo was being straight on this one."

Argyll, who brightened up quite considerably when he heard of Lorenzo's emotional entanglements, now began taking a more constructive part in the conversation.

"If Masterson was a protégée of Roberts, why was she about to sink her fangs into Kollmar, another Roberts' groupie?"

"Maybe she was interested in scholarship and just wanted to find out the truth?" Bottando commented dryly, in a way which suggested he thought this the least likely explanation.

"Maybe," Flavia replied, equally unconvinced despite her willingness to give the dead woman the benefit of the doubt. "If so, she was prepared to become very unpopular. Roberts wasn't pleased, nor was Kollmar. Miller disapproved and Van Heteren thought she was being silly. On top of that, even old Bralle had told her to lay off, according to one of the letters that Bovolo found in her papers."

She got it out of her folder and flattened it on the table. "It's in French," she said. "Thanking her for her letter, with a lot of scholarly guff to start off with. But the basic line is that Bralle reckons she is probably wrong in assuming Kollmar has made a mistake about this picture and will explain why when they next meet in Europe.

"In fact," she concluded, "the only person pleased was Lorenzo, who seems to be eyeing Kollmar up for the old heave-ho, although he basically confessed that he would much rather have got rid of Roberts."

Bottando eyed his empty plate nostalgically. "Which,

of course, he now has. Or someone else has for him. Charming or not, your Dr Lorenzo seems to be marching up towards the top of the likelies' list. He now has two vacant slots ready to be filled with his supporters.''

"But," Argyll objected, "you would have thought he would have waited until after Masterson delivered her promised knock-out blow to Kollmar. Then he would have had three slots free. Besides, it's rather an extreme way of winning votes, isn't it?''

Bottando sighed heavily at the ways of the world. "Ah, dear me. It always amazes me that people can use up so much energy fighting over so little. It sounds very much like the polizia.

"Now," he said, turning towards Argyll with a pleasant smile. "Mr Argyll. I trust you occupied yourself profitably this morning rather than brooding?''

Argyll gave a lengthy account of his activities in the library which produced a sort of glazed expression on Bottando's face.

"But what exactly have you found out?" he asked with a little impatience as Argyll clearly began to flounder.

"Well, firstly, the lovely Violante did leave Giorgione, probably for Pietro Luzzi, although not for long. She was buried the same year. And Titian and her brother Alfonso were clearly on very good terms. What I don't know is why Masterson was so concerned.''

"Yes. Yes. Most interesting," Bottando said uncertainly when the recitation came to a halt. "No great leap forward there, I see. So tell me about this committee instead. Does anybody pay much attention to these people? Is it worth all the sound and fury?''

"Of course it is," he replied in some surprise. "It's a high-prestige project. As you know very well, most pic-

tures are accepted as being by Raphael, or Titian, or
Rembrandt because experts say they are. Very few pictures have solid documentary evidence behind them. So,
if some reputable bunch weighs in with an opinion, then
it's taken seriously. Especially if it's got the official
stamp of approval from a government and vast amounts
of money to prove their accuracy. You know how easily
impressed some people are. So, museums eventually re-
label their pictures. Happily if a work is upgraded, with
much gnashing of the teeth and foaming at the mouth if
it's down-graded. I believe the catchword in America
these days is de-attribution.''

Bottando winced. He was something of a purist over
language, even other people's.

''And, of course, what these people say can make an
enormous difference to the price of the pictures if they
come up for sale,'' Argyll concluded.

''So, a proud owner who heard that his picture was
being de-attributed, if one must use that word, might react with some considerable anger. Even violence, one
might guess?'' Bottando asked, jumping at the chance of
a simple, straightforward motive.

''I suppose so,'' Flavia said reluctantly, rather regretting she had not thought of this. ''Better go and see the
owner of Kollmar's picture. Although in that case it
should have been Kollmar found with the knife in his
back, yet again. He was the one calling the picture a
fake.''

''We shall see,'' said Bottando with an air of finality.
''Time to go. I have to visit the Marchesa. It's what I'm
here for, after all.''

CHAPTER

8

Although obviously coming from one of those families which had hung on by their fingernails to social respectability since Napoleon invaded and destroyed the Venetian republic at the end of the eighteenth century, the Marchesa di Mulino still lived in some considerable state.

Old and battered her palazzo might have been, like its owner, but it was still worth a considerable amount of money. Most of the family pictures had long been dispersed, but Bottando's expert eye noted that what was left was of quite good quality. A little Tintoretto in the hallway surrounded by family portraits, a couple of what looked like Watteau drawings at the base of the staircase. Interesting point, that, he noted. And the usual tapestries, statuettes, and heavy sixteenth-century Venetian furniture. All in need of restoration but genuine stuff nonetheless.

She received him in bed. An old-fashioned touch, excused by her advanced age and the fact that she now rarely left the floor where the room was situated. The bed was gigantic, big enough for an entire family with room to spare, and the occupant was tiny, propped up by half a dozen embroidered pillows and looking like a neglected little doll. The old woman had a face that once upon a time had been beautiful; not handsome, or merely attractive, but ravishing. Even the lines and frailness of age could not conceal what once had been there.

And she had the manners of someone who was used to being deferred to and obeyed. She waved Bottando to a seat, as small for his bulk as the bed was big for hers, and looked him over carefully. No welcome, no thank you for coming. None of that. It was an honour for him to be allowed to see her, and he was not to forget it.

When she did finally speak, the impression of frailness was proven to be just that—an impression. Ancient though she was, there was nothing to suggest that her mind was anything but well-tuned. Nor had advanced years softened her view of the world.

"Come to find my little pictures, eh? All the way from Rome? And a full General as well? My goodness, what service we get from our police these days," she said with a little smile after the policeman had performed his introductory remarks.

"We try to please," he replied cautiously.

"Nonsense," she snorted. "Why else are you here?"

Bottando shook his head with indignation and a bit of surprise that she could apparently read his mind so well. "That's all," he said. "Just to find your stolen pictures. It's our speciality, you know."

She glanced at him slyly in a way which indicated she didn't believe a word of it, but let it go. "You're wasting your time," she said firmly. "If that's all you've come for, go back to Rome."

"We do have considerable expertise in matters of this

kind," Bottando said pompously. "We often pick up pictures when they are put up for sale."

"Nonsense," she repeated firmly. "Go home."

Bottando shifted uncomfortably on the seat, conscious of large portions of his anatomy hanging off the edges and wondering whether it could support him for long. He decided not to find out, and walked to the window clasping his hands behind his back.

"Oh, do stop wandering about, man," she said acidly. "If you're too fat for that seat, come and sit on the bed. Here," she patted the bed firmly.

Bottando had not been loosely attached to the army for nearly forty years without learning to obey commands. He did as he was told, conscious that this interview was not proceeding along orthodox lines.

"Well done," she said, patting his hand and smiling encouragingly as though he was a little boy who has successfully blown his own nose for the first time. "I suppose you need to ask lots of silly questions. Go ahead. You have five minutes. Then I have to sleep. I must have complete quiet."

"Well, then," said Bottando, still rather alarmed at his inability to get a word in, "why do you think we won't get them back?"

"Because you're idiots. All policemen are," she said confidingly, in case he might not be aware of the fact. "Not your fault, but there it is. Only fools want to be policemen."

It was a view Bottando frequently expressed himself, although it was disturbing to be included in the condemnation. Especially as it came from someone he was meant to be helping.

"But," he said, fighting valiantly, "what makes you think that the Englishman, Argyll, stole them?"

She laughed. "Him? Couldn't steal a packet of sweets from a shop. Lord, he even had trouble trying to buy them."

"But we had a complaint—"

"From Signora Pianta, no doubt. She would say that. She's a fool, too. A bit odd in the head, you know?" She squinted at him conspiratorially and dropped her voice. "Sees thieves, murderers and rapists everywhere. Comes of having a television in her room. Never watched one, myself. Do you have a television?"

Bottando was opening his mouth to confess that, indeed, he did have a set, although the pressure of work meant he rarely had time to watch it, when he checked himself and frowned. "As this theft was reported, we have to check it out, you know."

"She should never have reported it."

"Why not?"

"Scandal. Can't stand it. Won't stand for it. I refuse to see my name in the papers."

"Being robbed is hardly scandalous. It happens to all the best people, nowadays."

She sniffed. Evidently she thought that being robbed was a very bourgeois pastime.

"Who is this Pianta woman?" he asked. He had Argyll's description, but reckoned he was perhaps a little biased. No one could be that bad.

"My secretary, or companion, call her what you will. Hanger-on, basically. A distant relative, of the poorer variety. Dreadful woman, but useful for daily tasks. I'm used to her and I'm too old to change the people around me now. Besides, she annoys my interfering nephew even more than she does me."

He sighed heavily. "With your permission, I'll see how the pictures were taken out afterwards. Just in case.

I understand from Mr Argyll that someone else was also interested in buying them.''

She looked scornful again. ''Gibberish,'' she said firmly. ''Utter nonsense. Sounds like one of Pianta's little tricks again to get more money. No one has been interested in buying any of them for decades. Someone did write saying she wanted to examine one of the pictures, but there was no reason to think she was interested in buying.''

''She?''

''Oh, dear, you do go on,'' she said wearily. ''Very well, then. Bring me that cabinet over there.'' She gestured at what looked like a sewing box on the desk in the corner. Bottando got up thankfully from the bed and fetched it. She fished out an envelope and handed it over.

Bottando was pleased to see his assumption proved correct. It was a letter from Louise Masterson, postmarked from New York, asking for permission to photograph an anonymous portrait in the Marchesa's possession which she had noticed during a party thrown by Dr Lorenzo last year. She found the picture most interesting and would like to examine it under calmer circumstances. It was connected with a book she was planning to write.

''And you replied to this,'' he said.

''I told Pianta to write something, but I don't know if she ever got around to it. Stupid woman. She's not very efficient, you know, for all that she complains about everyone else.''

Bottando asked to keep the letter, then informed her he didn't think it likely that the woman would be keeping the appointment. She seemed untroubled by the news.

The conversation with Maddelena Pianta was less confusing, but also much less agreeable. Whereas the first was perhaps a little scatterbrained, she was lively, intelligent and had a sense of humour. At Bottando's expense, maybe, but she was clearly someone who had enjoyed her life and intended to have as good a time as possible in what little remained of it. Signora Pianta was the very opposite. Dour, humourless, suspicious, she did not appear to have had a good laugh since the early 1950s. And showed no signs of gearing up for another.

She answered Bottando's comments rapidly and with no elaboration whatsoever; yes, no, with everything else dragged out of her. She had accused Argyll, she said, because he was obviously responsible. He was a foreigner, wanted the pictures and objected to the price being asked.

Clearly, Argyll had made a bit of a hit here. Had she, he asked next, replied to Masterson's letter?

She was awkward and uncomfortable at the question, and then with obvious, although incomprehensible, reluctance admitted she had, to say that Masterson was welcome to see the picture if it had not been sold by the next time she was in Venice. She had phoned the fondazione on Friday morning to organise an appointment and had left a message with a functionary—she didn't know who but he seemed Italian—for Masterson to visit at nine that evening. She arranged to meet her on the Zecco, opposite the Giardinetti Reali and a few minutes' walk from the palazzo. That was because Pianta was going to the cinema and didn't want her arriving before she got back. Masterson had never turned up.

"I suppose you realise that while you were sipping your coffee and waiting, she was being murdered about a hundred metres away? It never occurred to you to report this?"

It had, she said, with an attempt at irritation to hide

her discomfort. But she didn't see what relevance it had. Besides, the Marchesa would have been furious at her getting involved in a scandal. No, she had seen no one acting suspiciously.

Bottando shook his head. Indeed, a silly woman. At least they now knew why Masterson was there. However, he was grudgingly forced to admit that it got them no nearer identifying the murderer. So he gave up, and told her she was obliged to make a formal statement on the matter. He tried to deal with her evident alarm by assuring her that there was no reason why it should ever feature in the newspapers.

The comment made her act a little more cooperatively, so he got her to show him where the pictures had once hung, and where, in her view, they were removed from the house.

The front door. Or rather, what had once served as the ceremonial entranceway from the Grand Canal, where the gondolas would pull up to let their passengers out with all due pomp and ceremony. Scarcely, if ever, used any more. The private gondola business is not what it was.

Bottando looked over the great door with a professional eye. Very old, perhaps eighteenth century, he thought. With wood that had been exposed to damp and heat continuously. Still very strong but held with a large and imposing lock that would have detained the average burglar for about thirty seconds. The same old story. What was the point of having heavy iron bars on all the windows if you leave the front door open?

While he was thinking, Signora Pianta told him in no uncertain terms that Argyll and his confederates—she still clearly saw him as some sort of latter day Raffles, which seemed to Bottando one of the most unlikely com-

parisons he had ever heard—must have come here in
dead of night, loaded the pictures up and sailed off to
hide them. No one had heard anything as most of the
bedrooms were on the third floor and the Marchesa habitually took a sleeping pill last thing at night. Bottando
grunted as she rattled on, opened the door and walked
out on to the landing stage.

There was a wonderful view up and down the canal,
despite the overcast sky. The white, wedding-cake-like
church of the Salute was immediately ahead, and he
could just see San Giorgio further out in the lagoon.
Boats of all sorts ploughed up and down the Grand
Canal, making waves which lapped up the wooden landing stage with a faint sloshing noise. A few multicoloured
umbrellas were still outside the cafés, bravely pretending
that summer was not yet over. The wind was fresh and
cold, coming in from the sea with that particularly tangy
smell that gave no idea of what a horribly polluted place
it really was.

A fairly busy part of the city, he thought to himself,
dragging his mind back to his duty. Could someone really
load up pictures and steam off with no one noticing?
Despite the enquiries of Bovolo's cohorts, they had as
yet found no witnesses. Amazing how few witnesses
there were to any aspect of this case.

"When was this entrance last used?" he asked, tap-
ping his foot on the frail wooden planks. "Officially, I
mean?"

"About a year ago. By Dr Lorenzo, the Marchesa's
nephew. He gave a party at the start of a meeting for this
new committee of his and arranged for everyone to be
brought in by boat. He and the Marchesa were in one of
their brief moments of talking to each other. It happens

about once a year, then they fall out again over the inheritance.''

He nodded absently and carefully studied the vast old piles of wood driven deep into the canal mud to hold the entire structure in place. Nothing noticeable. He pursed his lips as he thought, and then carefully examined the planking. Furrowed his brow to look thoughtful and marched briskly inside. He'd be back later, he said as he shook the woman's hand and prepared to go.

"So," he concluded later that evening. "We now know what Louise Masterson was doing wandering around that part of the city before she was killed. And we also have at last some firm links between this committee, the murders and these infernal pictures. That is, Lorenzo was to inherit them when the Marchesa died, Masterson was to look at one of them and someone else on the island knew · it. You would have thought," he said in passing, "that this little connection might have been discovered by your good friend and colleague Commissario Bovolo, but apparently not. Perhaps he thought it of no importance. Perhaps he is right."

He sipped his drink and looked thoughtful. "Where was I? Oh, yes. They all deny taking the message from Pianta or hearing anyone else on the phone. I rang them to check. Presumably at least one of them is fibbing a bit.

"Now, where exactly all this takes us is another matter, of course, but it represents a form of progress. I think." He was being modest. In reality, he was feeling rather pleased with himself.

"And you officially exonerate me from steaming off into the night with a boatload of paintings?" Argyll asked, relieved that he appeared to be fast coming off the wanted list.

"Oh, I think we can do that. Of course, we might have to arrest you as a diversionary tactic if we don't come up with anyone better before budget day, but I'm sure you'll understand," Bottando replied gravely. "Apart from anything else, no one steamed off into the night with them."

"I thought the door was opened," Flavia said, perusing the menu with great attention before ordering a *zuppa inglese* to fill up those awkward little coners.

"So it was. But that landing stage hadn't been used for a year. You can't load up a boat without making some scratches, or leaving some signs behind. And there was nothing at all."

"So how was it done?"

"Ah, well, that's a different question. All I know is what didn't happen. Ladies and gentlemen. Your thoughts, please?"

"What's the fight between the Marchesa and Lorenzo?" Argyll asked.

Bottando wagged his finger at him. "She can't disinherit him, if that's what you're thinking. The estate was left to him by his uncle, to be used by his wife during her lifetime. Which has, undoubtedly, proved longer than anyone expected."

"Any idea if Masterson's wanting to see this picture might have triggered her murder?"

"No."

"That phone call by Pianta to the foundation intrigues me," Flavia said, brow puckered as she counted through the options. "If the message was taken by one of Masterson's colleagues, that person would have known where to find her that evening. And therefore becomes an odds-

on favourite for the role of knife wielder. How many
people could be mistaken for Italian? Not Van Heteren
or Miller, who both have heavy foreign accents. Kollmar,
on a good day. Roberts certainly. And, of course, Lorenzo, although Pianta should have recognised his voice."

"True, but Lorenzo, it seems, wasn't there. That leaves
just Roberts, but Van Heteren says he was with him all
the time and insists he didn't speak to anyone. And I
can't see why he should want to lie about that."

"He would if he killed both of them."

"True. Very true. Maybe we should spend some time
checking his alibi a little more closely."

"I have," Flavia said. "Find me a way he could slip
out of a dinner party unnoticed for the hour and a half it
would need to cross Venice, kill Masterson and slip back,
and I will happily suggest he's our man."

They all paused for a moment to sip their drinks and
ponder the unfairness of life.

"While we're on the subject," she went on, "it is
quite possible to leave the Fenice, get to the garden, kill
Masterson and get back in time. But Frau Kollmar insists
neither Roberts nor her husband was out of her sight for
more than a few minutes."

Compared to Flavia's enthusiastic reconstructions of
possible scenarios and Bottando's successful interroga-
tion of Pianta, Argyll's own efforts seemed less than useful. He was, accordingly, a little shamefaced when asked
what he'd done that afternoon.

As he'd said to Flavia, his weakness as a dealer was
that he tended to get interested in the paintings he was
trying to buy. So it was with murder victims as well, it
seemed. He had rung up his employer, Sir Edward
Byrnes, and asked him about Benedetti, the owner of the

picture that caused the squabble between Masterson and Kollmar.

He'd also brought his employer up to date about his recent disappointments. Byrnes had conceded that these things did happen, although he had never heard of pictures being stolen at the last minute before. He urged Argyll to get back to Rome and start earning money again. This Argyll had promised to do.

"As for the picture, Byrnes knew nothing scurrilous about the owner at all and seemed very dubious about the idea of this man putting out contracts on art historians. But he said he'd have a sniff around. Apart from that, I decided it would be a good idea to go to Padua."

"Ah," said Bottando, taken by surprise. "Why do you say that?"

"Hagiography," he answered mysteriously. "Lives of the saints," he added, just in case the word was too long for them. "Flavia here says Masterson went to Padua last Thursday when she should have been at the committee meeting, and in the library she was reading accounts of Titian's frescoes in the Scuola di San' Antonio there. I thought it might be an idea to go and search for inspiration at the shrine of the saint."

"And what do you expect to find?"

He shook his head. "I don't know, really. Whatever Masterson found, I hope. She went there, announced she was going to rewrite her paper and was promptly done to death."

Bottando grunted that if Argyll thought the trip was worthwhile then he should naturally follow his instincts. Far be it from him to order him around. He clearly didn't feel there would be much point, and he had some doubts about Argyll's ability to discover one even if it existed.

Then he stumped off to bed and Flavia suggested a digestive walk.

They got lost again and were beginning to get thoroughly irritated by the refusal of Venice to conform to the normal layout of cities. Most, after all, are fairly straightforward: cathedral at one end, railway station at the other, everything else in between with taxis to ferry you around. Venice, alas, is not like that at all and, much as Flavia liked the place, it was making her increasingly frustrated. She had gone to see Bovolo, and got lost, then to see Lorenzo, and got lost again, now she was slowly going nowhere in particular and had got lost for the third time. It reminded her of her progress on this case a little too vividly to be comfortable.

Argyll, walking by her side with careless insouciance, didn't seem to mind as much. An incorrigible tourist, he spent his time craning his neck round looking at the buildings, trying every now and then to persuade her to stop talking and admire a church facade instead. She, in contrast, kept doggedly walking, fending off the feeling that she was doing little else but go round in ever diminishing circles.

"Here," she said eventually, thrusting the crumpled map at her companion. "I give up. Work out where we are and take me home."

He squinted at the map, looked around to try and find out the name of the alleyway they had stopped in. Then he turned it upside down and looked again, walked off, turned right and said: "How about that?"

She wasn't impressed. "This isn't the place," she observed tartly.

"I know that," he said, walking on to the high arched bridge leading to the other side of the little canal. "But it is where Roberts was fished out. That's not bad for a

start. We're not too far away. You can surely work out
the rest yourself. Roberts lived down that way,'' he said
pointing to his left. ''And the Grand Canal is that way,''
he added, pointing to his right.

''Which means that we''—he paused, thought, then
pointed again—''should go this way,'' he said, errone-
ously but with an air of triumph.

He handed the map back to her so that she could see
for herself what a magnificent navigator he was. While
she was admiring his confidence but doubting his conclusions, he took out his cigarettes. ''I knew I'd forgotten
something,'' he muttered, sticking his finger in the packet
in the vain hope that there might, perhaps, be one left in
there somewhere. ''Damn.''

He scrunched up the packet and tossed it casually over
the side of the bridge.

''Not very public spirited of you,'' Flavia observed.

He glanced down into the dirty water. The white crumpled packet was floating on the surface, surrounded by
half a dozen empty plastic bottles, what might once have
been a dead rat, several pages of newspaper and a motley
assortment of household garbage. They watched the collection drift slowly in the direction of the Grand Canal,
where it would undoubtedly join many more bits and
pieces before ending up in that great waste disposal unit
known as the Adriatic Sea.

''No,'' he said. ''Sorry about that.''

They watched the rubbish move slowly on the journey
for a few moments more. There was something . . . Then
Flavia said: ''It's going the wrong way.''

They examined it more carefully as it moved gently in
the direction of what was now downstream. ''So it is,''
he said after a while. ''The water was flowing away from

the Grand Canal last night, now it's heading towards it. Isn't that odd?''

"Flow," she said, with an air of certainty.

"Beg your pardon?"

"Nothing. How do you feel like going boating?"

It was not an invitation he'd expected; generally she was rather averse to fun and frivolity, at least while working. But who was he to dissuade her from taking an hour off? The timing was a little eccentric, though.

"Now? At eleven o'clock on a cold October night? What do you want? Gondola and bottle of wine?"

"Don't be absurd. No, I meant tomorrow. I'll organise it all. We can go when you get back from Padua." She paused and regarded him carefully before saying sternly, "Jonathan, do be careful."

It was a warning she gave fairly frequently when in his company. He had the habit of not really watching where he was going and crashing into obstacles, like lampposts and street signs, placed by local authorities trying to trip up the unwary. So it was now. Argyll had caught a glimpse of what appeared to be an unusually interesting statue of a saint picked out by the lights on the church of San Barnaba and had taken a couple of steps backward to improve his angle of vision. He was fond of statues of saints.

The manœuvre had brought his ankle into sharp contact with a concrete bollard, put there to inform the more normally observant that the canal was about to begin. As he was facing the wrong way, he now tripped, took another couple of steps back to regain his balance and vanished over the edge with a sharp cry of alarm that ended abruptly as his head disappeared, with a mighty splash, underneath the black, cold and smelly water.

Flavia ran to the side, fearing that yet another art his-

torian, even if a retired one, was about to be claimed by
the Venetian lagoon. She was worrying unnecessarily.
After a few seconds of thrashing around and cursing violently, Argyll stood up, knee deep in water and with an
embarrassed expression on what little could be seen of
his face. Apart from being imbedded in the thick and
slimy mud, soaked and feeling generally humiliated, he
appeared to have suffered little damage.

She giggled at the sight, then looked at him thoughtfully. "You OK down there?" she asked.

"Never better. How nice of you to ask. How are
you?" he replied, before slipping once more.

"The water's not very deep," she observed.

"You don't say."

"I mean, about a metre. There's not much chance of
your drowning, is there?"

He tried to wipe some of the mud off himself, and
shivered violently. "Not unless I try really hard, no. But
I might freeze to death. Will you stop talking and help
me out of here?"

"Oh, sorry." She rolled up her sleeve and held out a
hand with some distaste.

"What I meant," she went on as he clambered out and
she retreated upwind, "was that if you were in no danger
of drowning, nor was Roberts. If he slipped, that is. I
mean, he'd just have to walk to the side and hop out,
wouldn't he?"

She thought that was fascinating, and was going to
offer further observations, but the very nasty look that
Argyll gave her suggested he wasn't so interested at the
moment. So, keeping at a discreet distance, she accompanied him back to his hotel and ordered him a whisky
while he made an atrocious mess of the bathroom.

CHAPTER

9

At eight the following morning, General Bottando marched quickly up the steps of the carabinieri and headed for the office of Commissario Bovolo. He was not looking forward to the encounter.

Bovolo was, however, still in something approximating good humour. That is not to say that he actually smiled, or that his eyes danced with merriment, or anything like that, but rather that his morose air seemed to have lifted a fraction, a bit like a heavy sea fog that has just been touched by the weak rays of the winter sun. Clearly, Bottando thought, he is intoxicated with his success. Already imagining himself in his new job. He decided not to spoil the mood by recounting his discoveries.

"Do sit down, please," came the grey, monotonous voice as Bottando marched in. "I suppose you want my help."

The trouble with Italy's police force is that it is so fractured. In a more organised system, Bottando would have outranked this provincial little squirt by several degrees and could have insisted on full cooperation. With

awful penalties if it was not forthcoming. But, because
the police was split, his seniority counted for nothing.
Bovolo could throw him out, refuse to talk to him, anything he liked, and there was nothing the General from
Rome could do about it. A subordinate in the polizia who
talked to him in this vaguely insolent tone would have
been reprimanded sharply. With the carabinieri superin-
tendent, Bottando had no option but to react in a concil-
iatory fashion and nod meekly, especially considering his
weak position back in Rome.

"Something like that. It's about this theft of pictures."

Bovolo nodded. "I thought so. I reckoned you'd need
assistance. Curious, isn't it, the way we provincials manage to tie up a murder case within days and you experts
flounder around over a simple theft. As I say, it is what
comes of not having local knowledge. Still, that will all
be changing soon, eh?"

Bottando ground his teeth, and consoled himself with
the thought of all the explaining this horrid little man
would have to do if his half-formed theories proved to
be correct. He smiled grimly, and ploughed on: "Curious, indeed. Simple, it is not. Did you know that Louise
Masterson was interested in one of the pictures stolen?"

"No," he said without much interest. "Are you going
to tell me this concerns ghosts?" Bottando reckoned the
remark might have been a joke, so smiled.

"Hardly. But it is a coincidence. No matter. The point
is that I'm fairly sure that the robbery was a botched
job." Nothing of the sort, of course, but it would do.

"Why?"

"Because the thieves only stole very unimportant
paintings and left behind a Tintoretto, a couple of Wat-
teaus, and so on."

"Ignorant louts, no doubt. Southerners, probably."

THE TITIAN COMMITTEE   131

"The point is," Bottando repeated heavily, to get the meeting back on course, "that there is every likelihood they will come back once they realise they took the wrong pictures. It often happens, as I'm sure you know. And if that happens, and the Marchesa was attacked, or something like that, it would be most unfortunate."

That got him. Bovolo was envisaging a whole series of unfortunate consequences: Marchesa attacked, Bottando whispering into powerful ears, "Well, I did tell that man in Venice . . ." Not good for the chances of promotion.

"So, what do you want?"

"Well, I thought that you could station a man there for a few days. That would do fine. I'm sure the Marchesa would be most grateful."

She wouldn't, mind you; she'd be furious. That would be fine too. Bovolo, however, could only see her thanking him, inviting him to dinner, telling the powerful of Venice what a fine man he was. Just proved how little he knew her.

He was not, however, someone who even knew how to spell gracious, let alone act it. "Well," he said grudgingly, "we might be able to spare someone."

"Splendid. By the way, my assistant wanted me to ask you . . ."

Bovolo glared at him with fury. "Now listen here. This is quite enough. I must tell you, General, that I am getting very tired with your subordinate's interference. That woman is running around as though this was her own case . . ."

"You did ask her to talk to the members of the committee . . ."

"True. But I also told her to do nothing else. This case is closed and she is still bothering them. If this continues

I shall have to protest more officially. You keep her on the subject of thefts of pictures. Leave murders to people who know how to deal with them professionally."

Bottando held up his hands. "Don't worry, my dear sir," he said in a placatory fashion. "Point taken. Signorina di Stefano is here to help me find some pictures. I can assure you she will concentrate her mind solely on that."

Bovolo seemed mollified, and Bottando had got everything he wanted. So he thanked the miserable Commissario enthusiastically and lumbered off. He felt very pleased with himself. Not lost the old knack at all, he thought.

While Bottando was feeling pleased with his ability to manipulate men, Jonathan Argyll was wedged into a corner seat in a second-class carriage on the Venice to Padua train. It was very far from being an express service; the machine crawled and creaked its way through the flat and entirely uninspiring scenery to the west of Venice, stopping frequently at stations to unload passengers, pausing at others to pick up more and occasionally coming to rest in the middle of open countryside merely, it seemed, to get its breath back.

It was a dull and depressing trip that rather matched his mood. He had, so he thought, been quite good at keeping at bay his profound disappointment at recent events. But now, as he had nothing better to do, his mind went back over the whole business. And a miserable affair it was as well. He had lost his pictures; Bottando and Flavia were worried about their jobs; two people had been murdered, and they hadn't a clue what was going on or why.

For example, why was Masterson interested in that picture of his? Why had she rushed off to Padua only a few days before giving her paper? He liked to think that there was a connection, but he had no idea at all what it might be. Pleasant as it was to fantasise about lost Titian portraits, he knew very well that there was no chance that the Marchesa's work was one. Lorenzo was a close relation after all and, for all his frivolity, an expert on Titian; he would not miss something like that.

How Masterson knew about it was, at least, clear enough; she had been at the reception thrown by Lorenzo in his aunt's palazzo the year before at the start of her first committee meeting. She must have seen it then and remembered it. But what associations did it strike in her mind?

Whatever they were, it struck none in his, and he was in a thoroughly bad mood by the time the train eased into Padua station. He got out into the freezing cold and heard the rain pattering down on the glass roof of the shed. It had been threatening for days and had deliberately chosen the worst possible moment to unload. The weather had turned colder overnight. Indeed, as he'd noticed when he fell into the canal, it was pretty chilly before.

But now the combination of rain and icy air made the shortest moment outside miserable and he had not really come dressed for the occasion. He stood in the station lobby squinting up at the sky, hoping that he could will the clouds into parting, the rain into stopping and the sun into shining. All three ignored his wishes. He turned up the collar of his jacket as much as possible, stuffed his hands into his pockets, adopted an air of disgruntled suffering, and started walking. He hoped he was not about to go down with a stinking cold.

It was, damn the planners, a long way. Generally he was all for preserving medieval city centres and keeping modernity on the fringes. He was prepared to make an exception over railway stations on wet days, especially when the buses all seemed to have vanished and he was forced to march about a mile and a half to get to his destination. In such circumstances, knocking down a medieval church or two seemed a small price to pay for convenience.

After about thirty minutes of sacrifice to the causes of truth and justice he neared his journey's end, very much wishing that truth and justice would get on without him for a bit. The Scuola sat close to the cathedral, a drab building made even more unattractive by the voluminous pigeon droppings that turned much of its surface an unappealing off-white colour and made the statues on the main facade a little like religious snowmen.

But it was at least open. Too open, in fact. The wide doors faced directly into the wind and the air inside was, if anything, even colder and damper than the horrible stuff outside. He walked into the dark and windy building, stood uncertainly in the middle of the floor and looked around, unsure about what he was meant to do next. A helpful arrow pointed up the wide stone staircase, so he trudged upwards.

The paintings that he had vainly hoped might provide some sort of inspiration were at the end of the upper room, surrounded in heavy dark wood and greatly in need of restoration. Time, damp and lack of care had taken their toll. The paint had peeled off in several places, and the surface of the frescoes was very dark.

They were about as woebegone as Argyll felt and in truth, they hardly stood out as masterpieces of Renaissance artistic endeavour. Awkward, a bit stilted in their composition. Lifeless, in fact. By Titian, certainly, that was beyond doubt. But that merely proved that even the best painters had their off days. Maybe the great man had a headache. Or flu. Or perhaps he was as fed up as Argyll was now. He imagined the young painter, working away at his first real opportunity to show what he could do. On his own, with no masters or teachers breathing down his neck. He couldn't have been pleased. Surely, the artist knew in his heart he could do better than this.

Even the subject matter was very strange and elusive for someone like Titian, who generally preferred a very direct approach. After all, they were meant to celebrate the life of Saint Anthony of Padua, representing the great miracles he wrought. But in one of the pictures, the saint barely put in an appearance. And he wasn't exactly the centre of attention in the others, either.

Argyll consulted the little guide book he had brought with him. On the right, the *Miracle of the Talking Baby*, where an infant assures a doubtful husband, snappily dressed in a red and white costume, that his wife really is faithful to him. In the centre, the *Jealous Husband*, in which an aristocrat, evidently the same one judging by the clothes, stabs his wife to death in a garden, again because he thought she was unfaithful. She wasn't and, full of penitence, he comes to confess his sins to the saint, who raises the woman from the dead. Nothing like knowing when you've goofed. There's a point, though, he thought. Stabbed to death in a garden. Jealous man thinking she was unfaithful. Hmm.

"I said, can I help you?" said a man who had evidently been standing there for some time trying to attract his attention. Argyll leapt to one side.

"Oh," he said. "You surprised me," he added, stating the obvious.

The little man, who was probably a friar but more resembled a well muffled mole, looked at him curiously.

"You seem very interested in our building here," he said with a faint air of apology. "I was wondering if you needed any help. I would be quite happy to tell you about our treasures. These, as I'm sure you know, are by the great Titian."

Argyll mulled the offer over. The last thing he wanted was an extended guided tour in these temperatures. But he felt like talking to someone. He could hardly take this Franciscan to the local bar, though.

"Thank you. That's most kind of you to offer," he said. "What I'd really like to know is why St Anthony scarcely figures in pictures which are meant to be all about him?"

"Ah, well. A difficult man, Titian," the friar replied, talking about the painter as though he was a well-known local figure who could be seen dining out in restaurants most weekends. "But you know what artists are like. There are much more obvious scenes he could have chosen. I'm sure that caused annoyance, quite apart from the somewhat irreverent details about his mistress."

"What do you mean?"

"It's just a story, but it is said that Titian painted in the lovely Violante di Modena as the lady who gets knifed. Apparently, she was unfaithful and he wanted his revenge. The friars evidently thought this inappropriate, and I can't but agree with their judgement."

"Are you sure your storytellers aren't confusing him with Giorgione?" Argyll asked skeptically. "The unrequited love theme sounds suspiciously familiar. Besides, I thought she ran off with Pietro Luzzi, not Titian."

The little old man chuckled. "Ah, well. Maybe so. Like saints, the lives of painters get confused. Perhaps you are right, as I believe the lady was dead by the time he came here anyway. Historical accuracy, alas, does sometimes spoil a good story.''

"Do you know anything about the third painting?'' he asked, gesturing at the third panel. "It seems in a slightly different style to the other two.''

The friar inclined his head. "Very observant. The painter, I gather, wanted to do something entirely different which the chapter must have thought inappropriate.''

"What was that?''

"I don't know. It never got beyond the planning stage before the friars put their foot down and insisted on this one.''

"Most fascinating,'' Argyll said, as the man seemed to want encouragement. "I was most keen to see these pictures. I imagine you get a lot of tourists.''

"A fair number in the summer, yes. Of course, we are not as popular here as the Scrovegni Chapel down the road. Giotto seems to be a much bigger crowd puller. But we have our fair share.''

The little man smiled at his command of slang. "Not the best of times at the moment, of course,'' he went on. "Too cold and dark to see them properly. We had someone in here last week almost standing on the altar to get a good view. She was even using a flashbulb to take photographs. Of course, we are happy to allow visitors in, but we do rather disapprove of that sort of thing. Not respectful at all. And, of course, not good for the paintings. They're in bad enough condition as it is.''

"Some people are very badly behaved,'' Argyll said piously.

"Especially Americans. Not that they are bad people,'' he added hurriedly because of a sudden doubt about Argyll's likely nationality, "but they do tend to get over enthusiastic.''

"And this woman last week was an American?"

"Yes. Charming lady, when she got off the altar. Very knowledgeable and spoke good Italian."

"Did you tell her about the pictures as well?"

"Oh, there was no need to do that. I think she knew more than I did. But we had a very pleasant chat, until she had to run off on some important errands, and she was properly apologetic for getting on the altar. Left a very handsome donation in the box, as well."

Argyll thanked the friar profoundly for his help, ostentatiously emulated Masterson—it was obviously her, after all—by leaving a large gift in the money box and went to the nearest restaurant he could find. The question was, of course, what errands was she running?

He was back in Venice by the early afternoon and despite his misgivings, decided to be virtuous and not head straight for the bar of his hotel. It would have been a perfectly understandable decision. The wind was getting colder, the rain wetter and the temperature even lower. But the tides were behaving themselves and as the vaporetto ferried him slowly and choppily over to the Isola San Giorgio, he could see through the steamed-up windows of the ancient boats the white flecks of the waves on the usually calm surface of the water.

Even when he arrived at his destination, warmth and comfort were not his for long. His errand to Masterson's old room took only a few moments, after he had managed to negotiate his way round the porter who, fortunately, had evidently eaten much too good a lunch to be really on his toes about fending off interlopers. To get into Masterson's room he'd anticipated a lengthy process of easing off little wax seals put there by the police, but as they'd already dropped off, all he had to do was open the door and walk in, pick up what he wanted and scuttle out again. Silence in the corridor.

And then he was back outside. Again his selfless devotion to truth and his own income got between him and his hot bath. He crossed back to the main island and walked rapidly off in the direction of Masterson's last stand. He thought he might as well visit the scene of the crime. Not that he held out much chance of hitting, with eagle eye and triumphant swoop, on something the police had missed.

No, there was no doubt that his ambling around was due to a combination of voyeurism and indecisiveness, in more or less equal parts. The trouble was that he couldn't even work out where the murder had taken place. The machinery of investigation—tapes, little pointers stuck into the ground, armed guards and so on—had long since vanished, leaving only the grass, trees and a few greenhouses. And any clue would have been erased by the rain anyway, he thought, excessively conscious of how it was dribbling down the back of his neck.

The gardens were very striking, it had to be admitted, even though they showed unmistakable signs of end-of-season weariness, after months of hard pounding from the boots of tourists. The place was densely populated with trees and shrubs from both northern Europe and the Mediterranean, a horticultural metaphor for the city itself which had stood for centuries as the commercial link of east and west. Argyll peered around, and complimented the ancient gardener who shuffled past him. Just to pass the time of day.

This latter brightened noticeably. Thanked him, in fact, and said not many people appreciated his efforts. Argyll said the layout was truly magnificent. The old man nodded sagely and, mutual sympathy established, invited him into the warmth of the greenhouse to admire his work more closely. They walked into the humid and warm building shivering, and the man produced a bottle of grappa from a sack of manure. It kept the alcohol warm, he explained as he unscrewed the cap, and Argyll gratefully took a sip of the fiery liquid.

He gazed in respectful silence at the multicoloured display, now beginning to fade very noticeably, that lay before them.

"Wasn't that woman killed somewhere around here?" he asked. "I hope she didn't cause too much damage to your plants." Thinking about it later it seemed a fairly callous thing to say.

But to the gardener Argyll had his priorities entirely right. It was regrettable to be murdered, he seemed to think, but that was no reason to be inconsiderate. Just because you're dying doesn't give you the right to make a mess of flowerbeds.

He didn't quite say that, but from the disgusted way he pointed at a bed on the left of the little greenhouse, his feelings were entirely clear. Did Argyll have any idea of the difficulty of getting lilies to grow? Or how expensive each individual plant was? The Englishman confessed he had not a clue, but imagined that it was a job only a true expert could pull off.

"That's right, sir. That's right. You're a gardener yourself, I've no doubt. Ah, all the English are gardeners, so you will know. Come here."

And he grabbed hold of Argyll's elbow and dragged him along the narrow corridor. "Look," he said.

It was a bit of a mess. A rectangular bed, about three times as long as it was wide, full of lilies. Rather a pretty display, in fact, had not a broad swathe been cut straight down the middle, flattening most of the plants and leaving only a few pathetic remnants standing.

"Dear me, dear me," Argyll commented sympathetically. "What a dreadful thing."

The gardener nodded fervently. "That's right. Twenty-eight plants. And lilies as well. The noblest of flowers. Symbol of the kings of France, did you know that?"

Argyll confessed that he had heard of it. He stood, hands in pockets, and regarded the devastated flowerbed before him. It made him feel uneasy, for reasons he couldn't quite place.

So he bade the gardener farewell, and wished him good fortune in the next growing season, receiving in reply the grumpy assertion of belief that his flowers would no doubt be picked by tourists or succumb to disease. And then, at last and with only a small diversion, to his warm and cosy hotel room, where the hot water ran freely, the pot of tea was comforting and Flavia had left a note for him demanding his immediate presence. He cursed her roundly, and headed off into the cold once more.

CHAPTER

10

She was sitting, wrapped up in the waterproof clothes she had brought with her from Rome, in an old boat by the Accademia bridge. The rain was still drizzling down and it was getting late; there was only about another hour before the autumn darkness would make it difficult to see anything at all. Beside her, sitting and talking volubly, was an old walnut of a man, his hands flailing through the air as he chattered away. Even from a distance, Argyll could see that Flavia was being sweetly polite, as she always was with her elders, no matter how irritating she found them. As he approached, he thought he made out the words, "Flow. That's what it is, flow . . ."

He greeted them from the quay, and gingerly made his way down into the little boat. The last thing he wanted was to fall into the water again. Flavia introduced the old man as Signor Dandolo, a retired gondolier she had met a few days earlier.

Argyll shook the man's hand. "Signor Dandolo. You have a very distinguished name," he commented. A fine compliment, and well received. Dandolo beamed at him.

"That's right. Doges several times over in my family. Venetians since time began."

A little exaggeration here, surely, but no matter. Dandolo was pleased and Flavia was in the good mood that came over her when she felt she was doing something useful. Only Argyll felt thoroughly discontented.

"This is not my idea of a romantic boating trip," he grumbled as he drew his coat closer round him to fend off the chill evening air. "I'm soaked and it's bloody freezing. I'm not expected to burst into song, am I?"

Flavia ignored the remark, frowning as she looked ahead to see where they were going. She clutched the side of the boat quickly as a vaporetto ploughed past and the wake made their little skiff rock from side to side.

"You're not seasick, are you?" he asked incredulously.

She shook her head with determination, but kept her mouth shut. The frown deepened. "Indigestion," she said faintly after a while. "Must have eaten too much."

Impossible. She was seasick. Amazing. Twenty metres from the side of the Grand Canal and she was turning green already. Argyll shook his head and looked at the view. There was little else to do; Flavia was not at her conversational best. So he talked to the steadily rowing Dandolo, who glanced sympathetically at Flavia. She had won an admirer.

Like many Venetians, he was concerned to defend his city against the suggestion it might have any little flaws. The rough waters and inclement weather, he explained, were entirely unnatural for the time of the year. This was the first rain for weeks. Dry as a bone until then. Not a drop. He hinted that the rain was also the fault of the city planners, Romans and Milanese to a man. It had not rained, he seemed to imply, in the days of his ancestors, the doges.

After about ten minutes hard rowing, Dandolo swung the boat sharply to the left and propelled it at high speed down the rio di San Barnaba, past the site where Roberts was discovered. The swell of the water eased off noticeably and, by the time they reached the spot where Argyll had taken his plunge the night before, Flavia's complexion, if not back to its usual healthy tan, had at least lost the jaundiced hue so apparent on the Grand Canal. It was replaced by a return of her conversational powers.

"Flow," she said when finally prepared to answer Argyll's question about the point of the trip. "The current was reversed. Signor Dandolo here reckons it's because of new channels dug in the lagoon. The young policeman that Bovolo shut up realised it as well. So, instead of Roberts falling in near the Grand Canal, he must have dropped in a couple of hundred metres in the other direction. And, as you demonstrated last night, he couldn't have drowned accidentally."

"He could if he was unconscious."

"Or if he was held under the water. But how do you do that in one of the most crowded parts of Venice without anyone noticing? Answer, a couple of hundred metres up the canal is Roberts' house. There, in fact," she said, pointing with one hand and hanging on to the side of the boat with the other.

The house was on the corner with a little alley just past a bridge. The street along the rio di San Barnaba had given out by that stage, so the building backed straight on to the canal. Dandolo stopped rowing and the boat slid quietly along.

"Now what?" Argyll asked. It was all very interesting, but he didn't really see why they couldn't have found this out from their hotel. "What's that, by the way?"

"That" was a dark hole at water level which disappeared underneath the house.

"Covered canal," Dandolo said. "There're hundreds of them. For sewage. You can also run a boat in. That's how you get furniture in and out. And refuse, of course, sometimes."

"Can you get us in?" Flavia asked a bit half-heartedly.

Dandolo turned the boat, headed it straight at the hole and at the last moment shipped the oars. The boat slid in with a few inches to spare on either side.

"I knew this torch would come in useful," Flavia said, fishing around in her handbag.

"You don't have a couple of gas masks in there as well, do you?" asked Argyll plaintively. The smell was indeed fairly remarkable, although considering they were sailing down an open sewer serving half a dozen or more houses, it was no more than should be expected.

"It should widen a bit shortly," said Dandolo, who appeared entirely unaffected. "There. Told you."

He was, they dimly saw in the almost complete dark, correct. Flavia switched on the torch and moved the beam around. They were in a low, vaulted, brick tunnel, and to their right was a small landing stage. In the far wall was a door.

"Could you pull over there?" she asked the boatman, and he patiently complied. Flavia stood up as the boat nudged against the stone flagging and, hanging on to Argyll to keep her balance, eased herself on to the jetty.

"God, this is repulsive," she said in a disgusted tone which echoed bleakly down the dark and damp tunnel. "It's covered in green slime. Smells worse than you did last night."

"Don't worry, the rain will wash it off. Why don't you stay in the boat? You can see as well," Argyll asked, considering, then rejecting, the idea of following her.

"Because I'm looking," she said absently, crawling around on her hands and knees and playing the light of the torch around. She took a handkerchief out of her pocket, stood up as best she could in the circumstances and wiped some of the green slime off her knees. She eyed the result with disgust.

"Do you have any idea how much these trousers cost?" she asked rhetorically. "Look at that. Ruined. The things you do. If I weren't so good at this job I might seriously consider going off to do something a little more dignified."

"Does that mean you've found something?"

"Of course I have." She shone her torch from the doorway to the side of the canal. "Something—or rather someone—was dragged along here not very long ago. Guess who?"

"Roberts?" he suggested, with no great display of genius.

"Just so," she said with satisfaction, reaching into her handbag once more and producing a small camera. "It would be better to have professional snaps," she said as the flashgun went off, "but these will have to do for the time being. Bovolo would complain about interference again. Last thing I want is for him to start up. He's already refusing to give Bottando information I wanted."

"How about fingerprints?"

She shook her head. "Not my area of expertise, but I doubt it very much. The surface is too rough to hold them. Ah, well. Can't have everything. Do you fancy an impromptu visit to Professor Roberts' house?"

In fact, that proved impossible. The door which, she

confidently told him, led into Roberts' cellars, was firmly locked and Argyll was unwilling to try to kick it down, despite her encouragement.

"Are you mad? It's solid oak and about a foot thick. Besides, I'm cold."

He was right, although Flavia, who was enjoying herself enormously now that her sickness had passed off, considered him a bit of a kill-joy. She reluctantly levered herself back into the boat and Dandolo began the process of reversing the boat back into the canal.

"That's clear, anyway," Flavia said decisively. "We can scrub the accident theory."

"You reckon."

"I reckon. Roberts gets a visit from Masterson's killer. Roberts accuses him, and whoever it is decides he has to be shut up. He grabs him by the neck, hence the red marks. Down to the cellar and on to the jetty, holds him under the water until he drowns and then trots off home for dinner. Roberts, meanwhile, drifts off into the sunset until found by Bovolo and his mob. Simple."

"OK, then. Now for the difficult ones. Who, why?"

Flavia shrugged, and fell silent.

Argyll shivered once more. "That phone call? Roberts took it, Van Heteren overheard, and was afraid Roberts might tell us?"

"Maybe. The old Crime of Passion scenario again. Still the problem of his alibi, of course."

"Kollmar, then? He was here at about the right time?"

She shrugged non-committedly. They were back on the canal and the wind was picking up. He studied the sky. "Dammit, it's still raining," he said.

Dandolo grunted as he pulled on the oars. "That's right," he said. "Going to get worse, as well. Could flood if it's heavy enough. Depends on the wind when it's high tide on Sunday. Do you want me to take you back to your hotel?''

The thought of bobbing in his tiny boat all the way along the Grand Canal terrified both Argyll and Flavia equally. They assured him simultaneously that it was quite all right and they'd taken up far too much of his time already and he shouldn't even think of it. So he dropped them at the Ca' Rezzonico vaporetto stop, Flavia handed over generous amounts of money, and he disappeared into the darkness and drizzle, weaving in and out of the heavy traffic of the canal.

''How was Padua?'' she said as the little boat vanished in the gloom.

Argyll shrugged. ''I don't know really. Masterson was there, certainly. What she was doing is another matter. She had important errands, she said, but I've no idea what they were. I'm beginning to get a feeling, though . . .''

Flavia looked concerned. Argyll's theories were dangerous, not least because they tended to be wrong for the first half dozen tries. ''What is it then?''

The boat came and they got on, and Argyll changed the subject. It was not that he didn't want to say, he explained, it was just that he had little to go on and she always tended to be rather severe with him when he got it wrong. So if she didn't mind . . .

Flavia did mind, although she could hardly blame him. Anyway, the afternoon had been fairly successful and she was looking forward to presenting Bottando with her conclusions. So she forgot the matter, and went back to her hotel while Argyll trotted off in the other direction to do a little shopping.

•   •   •

Friday brought another train trip. Originally, Bottando had proposed going with Flavia himself, leaving Argyll behind to do whatever it was he thought art dealers did with themselves in their idle moments. However, the little excursion to Venice had already taken up more time than he liked and, as he kept on mentioning to the point of obsession, it was budget season. Tables of statistics had to be prepared, bureaucrats buttered up, past triumphs listed and mishaps carefully hidden from view. So, with much reluctance and even more preparatory doses of aspirin, he set off in great ill-humour to return to his desk in Rome.

Why didn't Flavia take Argyll with her, he had suggested with what appeared to be a knowing look before he went? It had always been one of his little illusions that, in that pair, lay a great love affair waiting for the appropriate circumstances to surface. To Flavia that had always seemed less than likely, mainly due to Argyll's chronic indecisiveness. But it pleased Bottando to take an avuncular interest in these matters, and she felt disinclined to spoil his romantic notions.

Argyll was quite happy to go, as long as they went by train and not by car. Otherwise, he said, he would stay where he was. Although she had not yet involved him in a crash, and indeed was an extraordinarily accurate driver, he was pusillanimously convinced that it was only a matter of time. High speed is an exhilarating thing, and Flavia's habit of looking deep in your eyes when talking to you was charmingly appealing. Both at once was not, to his mind, the happiest of combinations.

Flavia, of course, thought going by train not nearly as much fun, but fell in with his wishes. So they took the ten o'clock express, occupied the first-class seats she had booked and, at her not entirely unforeseen suggestion, immediately abandoned them in favour of the restaurant car.

They ate in companionable silence and after the last crumb had vanished, Argyll sprang his little surprise, the one he had been thinking about since the previous evening. He took out Masterson's photographs of Padua developed from the film he had removed from her camera yesterday.

"Hmph," she said after studying them for a moment. She always said that when she knew she was meant to say something intelligent but couldn't think what it was.

"Surely you can do a bit better than that," Argyll said in a slightly disappointed tone. "Do you want a hint?"

She clearly did, so he went on: "The face in the two pictures painted by Titian in Padua is the same as the self-portrait of the Marchesa's. I thought you would have seen that immediately."

"So I might have done, if I had seen this mysterious portrait," she replied snappily. "Anyway, so what?"

Argyll was a little crestfallen, considering that he had immediately assumed it to be of vast significance. There was certainly no room for doubt at all. The beaky nose, thin cheeks and lank hair were confirmation enough. What he didn't understand was why she wasn't all excited.

"But don't you see? It explains why the picture was stolen."

"I don't see that. It demonstrates that four hundred years ago there was a connection between the two pictures and you can assume that Masterson knew it. I can't see what else it shows. Unless you are going to suggest the Marchesa's picture is a Titian self-portrait."

"No. It's certainly not. We know very well what he looked like."

"So where does that get us?"

"I thought it was rather interesting . . ." he began.

"No doubt. And normally I'd agree with you. But there isn't time for that sort of thing at the moment. You will have to drop everything not connected to this murder."

"It is connected to the murder, I think," he protested.

"Maybe. But you don't know what the connections are."

Argyll shook his head. "Well, not yet," he admitted. "You're sometimes very demanding, you know. I thought I was being very helpful."

"And so you are," she replied in a most irritating fashion. "It's just that I was imagining Bottando's face if he heard all this. All he would say is: 'Who killed Masterson and Roberts, who stole the paintings and where are they, and where's the proof?' We don't know."

"I think you're being most ungrateful," Argyll sniffed in a hurt manner. "When all my research leads inevitably to the correct identification of the felon, I might very well keep the information to myself."

Flavia grinned broadly at him and patted him on the back. "Nonsense. You'll rush round and tell me. I know you. And I don't mean to be discouraging. But your task is to find those pictures. I very much hope you do, but you're nowhere near yet."

True enough, and the memory of his employer, sitting in London and presumably getting ever more impatient for results, put him into a reflective reverie for the next half-hour. Then, to pass the time as the train whistled through the flat, boring Veneto plain and moved into the flat, boring Lombardy plain, he took out his book. He had brought with him a detective novel of immense frivolity, but Flavia confiscated it.

"Read this instead," she said, handing over Master-son's work on Renaissance iconography. "It's good for the soul."

"Must I?" he asked plaintively.

"Yes. It would take me weeks to plough through that much English. Flick through it and tell me what you think. It won't take you long."

He eyed it suspiciously. It was awfully long, and he noticed with irritation that Flavia had bought herself a much more interesting magazine to wile away the time. He looked at the pictures, which was the bit he always enjoyed best, and then reached over to pick up a ticket stub that fell out of the middle.

"She got around in her last days," he observed.

"Mmm?" Flavia said inattentively, engrossed as she was in her horoscope, which was confidently predicting dire financial troubles mingled with exciting romantic en-tanglements for one twelfth of the world's population over the next thirty days.

"She arrived in Venice by train from St Gall. Where is St Gall?"

"Switzerland, I think," she replied. "What's your sign?"

"Leo," he said. "Why would she go to St Gall?"

"Leo? Are you sure? You're meant to be aggressive and determined. It's on the shores of Lake Constance. Nice place. Maybe she just wanted a day's rest to prepare herself. Like Miller and his swimming."

"What do you mean, 'meant to be'?" he said huffily, but she didn't reply. Nor did she tell him what the stars had in store for him that month.

At the great station in Milan, Flavia hailed a taxi with a whistle that made it sound as though the days of steam trains had returned once more, and they headed off through the busy and noisy streets to Benedetti's apartment. Argyll felt oddly uncomfortable until he realised that, even after only a few days in Venice, he had got used to not seeing, hearing, smelling or avoiding cars everywhere he went. A lot to be said for canals after all.

Signor Benedetti was a bit crumbly and, in the fashion of the elderly, fast asleep in his post-prandial nap when they entered. His maid gave him a good shake to bring him round. He yawned, and blinked, and rubbed his eyes as she explained who the visitors were and reminded him that they had an appointment. Then she helped him out of the old leather armchair and he hobbled over to greet them, burbling apologies for his discourtesy in not being better prepared for their arrival.

"That's quite all right," Flavia assured him. "It's very good of you to see us at all at such short notice."

"Good heavens, my dear young lady, I am delighted. An old man like myself rarely has the opportunity to welcome young people into his house. Especially beautiful young women like yourself."

No mention of handsome young men, Argyll noted. Ah well. At least he paid his compliments with decorum. No slobbering over hands or any nonsense like that.

They sat down, Argyll and Flavia on a thin-legged and rather insubstantial *settecento* sofa, Benedetti in the much more voluminous leather armchair. Both of the visitors studied their host carefully as the maid, who appeared to double up as a nurse, arranged a heavy woollen blanket around him. He was probably in his eighties. Not very well preserved, but evidently looked after himself well. A wizened and cherubic old face that the shrinkage of the years had made to look several sizes too big for the little body underneath it. When he was all tucked in and comfortable, he looked steadily at them both, waiting for them to begin.

Flavia explained how Masterson was murdered while doing some work on the old man's painting. He nodded quietly and listened to her patiently. He was most distressed to hear it, he said quietly. A charming woman.

"You met her, then?"

Indeed, he said. She'd paid a brief visit the previous week. His friend Georges Bralle wrote to introduce her and he was more than happy for her to come. Especially as she was interested in his pictures.

"I am very proud of my little collection, even if that committee was less impressed. A great shame that."

"Do you know Bralle well?"

"Not well. When I thought of selling the sketch a couple of years ago Georges suggested I consult his committee officially. That, of course, was before they had a fight and he retired in protest."

"They had a fight?"

"Something like that. Maybe not. Georges was always a bit prickly about that committee. Tended to regard it as his personal property. I'm sure it was all his fault. Charming man, but a bit difficult."

"So did you consult the committee?"

"I did. And eventually Professor Roberts came to see it."

"And he said he believed your work was not by Titian?"

"Not at all. He made it clear it was only a preliminary visit and that follow-up examination by a colleague was necessary. But I reckoned by his reaction that he thought it was very much genuine, especially when I showed him the documentary evidence Bralle had sent me."

Now this was a puzzle. No one had mentioned documentary evidence before. Quite the opposite. "What are you talking about?"

"Georges sent me various gleanings from his research over the years—when he remembered—I haven't actually seen him for a decade or more. You know, fragments from here and there. He never studied the picture particularly, but would occasionally come across a little snippet and send it. Taken altogether I thought it looked quite impressive. On the desk," he said, gesturing in that direction.

Flavia went and picked up a file he had brought out in preparation. Clearly he was acute enough to work out what they were coming for. She glanced at the contents—the letter of introduction from Bralle, sale contracts from the 1940s, cleaning and framing bills and so on. Nothing else. She pointed this out.

"Oh, silly me. Of course, I gave it all to Professor Roberts to hand over to his colleague."

"So what went wrong?"

"I don't know. Roberts said that side of things would be handled by his colleague, who would draw up the final report, incorporating his own findings. Evidently this man didn't find the evidence convincing enough. I was most disappointed, I can tell you, as was Georges when I told him the result."

"And what did Dr Masterson think?"

"I don't know that either. She said she would tell me later, when all her work was done. We didn't discuss it for very long. I'm afraid I talked too much. I don't get many visitors these days, and when I do I get carried away. I must have bored her dreadfully with my little anecdotes, but she didn't admit it. She sat and listened to me for a long time, and even missed her train. Very kind, I thought."

"So she didn't see any documents?"

"I offered to get her copies, but she said she didn't need them. I was a little surprised, I must say."

"When Dr Roberts was here, what did you talk about?"

He thought again, and remained silent for an alarmingly long time. Eventually, he nodded slowly to himself as he pinned the memory down. "Most of the time, nothing. I showed him the picture and left him alone with it. That took about an hour. Then I gave him a drink, he declined my offer of lunch and he went. We spent some time discussing my wish to sell the picture."

"In what way?"

"Obviously, I said I rather hoped he would report the picture to be genuine because I wanted to sell it. He said that he would do what he could. He was most helpful. After the committee voted against it, he wrote apologising for what he said was a piece of bureaucratic silliness and offered an attribution based on his own authority until it was all sorted out. With, of course, a fee of five per cent on the sale price. I gather that is a normal way of proceeding. I consulted Georges, who suggested I wait to see if the committee changed its mind. So I turned it down. It was tempting, but I wasn't in that much of a rush to sell."

Argyll felt his mouth sagging open in astonishment. He glanced at Flavia, but she seemed as calm and unconcerned as ever, so he bided his time.

"Perhaps you might want to see this famous work?" the old man went on. "It seems a pity to come all this way without looking at it."

Both nodded with enthusiasm at the idea, and Benedetti slowly eased himself out of his seat, Flavia helping on one side and Argyll on the other. When he was set

upright and balanced, he slowly led the way into what
he called his cabinet, a small study where he kept his
smaller pictures.

It made Argyll's heart burn. What he would do for a
room like this! Delicate plaster ceiling, marble fireplace
with logs burning gently in it, dark, well-polished oak
shelves supporting thousands of leather-bound books.
Light, warmth, a feeling of well-packed comfort. And
pictures, several dozen of them, of high quality, arranged
in the old style, one above the other, with none of the
modern sparse, spotlit fastidiousness.

"Beautiful," he said. "Absolutely beautiful."

Benedetti smiled appreciatively at him. "Thank you.
Without any modesty at all, I must say you are quite
right. It is my favourite place in the world. I am never
happier than when I am sitting in here. I shall be sorry
to leave it. Alas, I don't expect heaven will have anywhere half as nice, even if I am lucky enough to get in.
There it is, by the way."

He pointed shakily to a picture hanging between the
windows, sandwiched between a small seventeenth-
century Flemish interior and what appeared to be an
eighteenth-century French landscape.

It was a fairly innocuous scene. A man in a red and
white striped outfit with a beaky nose was sitting at a
table, on which there was a pile of food, wine and large
flowers. He was surrounded by three other people, one
dressed as a friar, and on the far wall was a carving of
the crucified Christ. The subject's hands were folded over
his stomach. Angels, as they do sometimes, were flying
around the room blowing trumpets. A perfectly normal
scene of everyday life in the sixteenth century. It was
painted in thick, heavy brushstrokes as though done in a
hurry. Clearly a sketch for a finished painting.

"Well, Jonathan, this is your area. What do you think?"

Argyll stared at the picture, ever more amazed. What on earth were these people playing at? He shook his head in confusion. "I don't understand this at all," he said.

Both of his companions eyed him curiously. "I mean," he said, "I can't see that there is any doubt about it. It is so obviously a preliminary sketch for one of the panels in the Padua St Anthony series; I don't understand why there was any doubt."

"Are you certain?" Flavia asked, impressed by his confidence. "After all, you're no Titian expert yourself."

"Yes. Firstly, Titian, it seems, painted a sketch of a scene for the series which was rejected by the friars. So he did another. This has the right proportions. The colouring is right, the style is right. St Anthony was a friar, as is this character here. In all three pictures the central character wears a red and white striped outfit. I'm sure this is the *Miracle of the Meal*. If your lives of the saints are a bit shaky, St Anthony was at a dinner where the host tried to poison one of the guests. St Anthony's presence made the poison harmless, and everybody felt awfully guilty and repented of their sins. You know the routine."

Benedetti nodded in agreement. "Very learned, young man," he said, unaware that Argyll had got it out of a cheap guidebook bought the previous day. "However, there is one little snag. As Dr Masterson noticed, the whole point about the legend is the guest ate the poison happily, 'praising God in his heart.' This man seems decidedly ill. Besides, there's the little inscription at the bottom. The Book of Job, I believe. *Homo igit Consutu* . . . 'A man dies and he disappears.' Hardly appropriate for a miracle of salvation."

They all advanced on the picture and stared at it closely. Undoubtedly the old man was correct; those around the central figure, as much as they could be distinguished, seemed more jubilant than awestruck. And the guest himself did not look at all like someone who had just been given an indisputable sign of Divine protection. In fact, he looked very poorly indeed, with a thin, pallid face accentuated by straight dark hair and a look of anguish that emphasised the somewhat sharp nose.

"Hang on a second, there. Flavia. Isn't that hooter familiar, somehow?" Argyll whipped out his collection of photographs once more and laid them out on the rosewood desk. Pretty convincing.

"There," he said. "Proof positive, or pretty nearly. The guest is the same person as the murdering husband in the other scene. And, incidentally, the same as the figure in the Marchesa's portrait. That's why Masterson couldn't be bothered with documentary evidence. She didn't need it. That's why she went to Padua.

"I don't know what you will think of this," he went on with a sudden and unexpected burst of dynamism, "but I work as the Italian agent for Byrnes Galleries in London. If you want to sell this picture, I will take it. Flat commission charge or percentage, and I can guarantee it will get a very good price. And no fee for authentication. With all this, it scarcely needs it."

Benedetti thought for a while, and then nodded. Old, but fast on his feet where money was concerned. Once a banker, always a banker. Must be the Lombard air. "That sounds an interesting proposition. You will have to take care of all the documentation and preparation and all that. I will send you a letter detailing my requirements, and you can send a provisional contract for my lawyer. No sale as a Titian, no fee. Is that right?"

Argyll nodded, wondering if he was going too far, and surprised that the man had turned out to be so decisive. At the very least he expected several weeks of protracted negotiations. But he had rarely felt so convinced of anything, certainly not a picture. "Agreed. And I shall be collecting my fee. Of that I am sure."

Flavia coughed gently to indicate that she was still there. "I hate to interrupt, but we are here on a murder investigation, not a picture buying expedition. And I'm not too sure of the proprieties of buying and selling what might turn out to be evidence."

Argyll grinned happily. "Sorry about that. But it takes so long to organise sales these days that I'm sure this case will be over before it goes ahead."

"Not too long, I hope, young man. Remember, I am old, and have descendants to worry about."

"Tell me about Georges Bralle. Where does he live?" Flavia asked to get the discussion back on more appropriate lines.

"In the south of France. He went to live in his little house there when he retired. He almost never leaves it. Why do you ask?"

Flavia shook her head. "Because he did leave it not very long ago. That letter of introduction for Masterson was written from a hotel in St Gall, Switzerland, on the day Masterson herself was there. For someone who has retired from the committee, he keeps in close contact. I thought it might be quite interesting to hear what he has to say. An informed outside view, so to speak. Do you have a phone number?"

Benedetti looked apologetic. "I'm afraid you will find him a difficult man to talk to. He has no telephone; always disliked them and now he's retired he indulges all his little whims. He has never really approved of the twentieth century. A very good letter writer, but that might not be fast enough for you.''

He gave her the address while Flavia asked him if he would be prepared to make a formal statement about what he had told them. He said he would, of course, be delighted, and they left. Outside once more she hailed a taxi and told the driver to go to the nearest car rental company as quickly as he could manage.

''I don't like the sound of that. Where are we going?''

''France,'' she said. ''Or more particularly, Balazuc. A village in the Ardèche, I believe. About a nine-hour drive. We can be there by tomorrow, then fly back from Lyons to Venice. Very dramatic and a thorough pain in the neck, but no choice.''

Having ended up in the one position he hoped to avoid—
that is, on an Italian motorway and in the passenger seat
of an Alfa Romeo with Flavia driving through the Friday
rush-hour traffic—Argyll tried, nonetheless, to keep himself calm and collected. He quietly recited a prayer for
the dead as she settled the car down at a steady one
hundred and sixty kilometres an hour, but apart from her
habit of using both hands to light her innumerable cigarettes, she did relatively little to make his incantations
necessary. She was a very good driver. It was everyone
else on the road that worried him.

He was, in any case, still quite impressed with the way
he had grabbed the opportunity which presented itself in
Milan, and Flavia was equally congratulatory.

"But are you sure it's the real stuff?"

He nodded firmly. "Absolutely sure. Feel it in me
bones."

"Don't see that it's conclusive, though."

"It's not. That's why I'm happy to go with you to see

Bralle. I want to see whatever evidence it is that he dug up.''

"But why is the man so miserable when he's meant to be beatific?"

The problems of scholarship. "I don't know. All these questions. All I can say is that Masterson was convinced and I'm willing to take a bet on her judgement. And on that of Bralle and Roberts, come to think of it. It's just a pity she's not around to give us a little hint. The question I'm more worried about is why did Kollmar, alone of everyone who'd studied it, disagree? And then say Roberts told him it was a dud when Roberts had told you and Benedetti pretty much the opposite? And why did Bralle say Kollmar hadn't made a mistake?"

"Tell me."

"I don't know. Finally, what about Roberts' disgraceful behaviour to Benedetti?"

"Eh?" she asked absently, undertaking a truck then pulling out to pass a BMW, whose owner resented it and gave chase. "What do you mean?"

"The cut. Roberts offered Benedetti an authentication in exchange for a cut of the sale price when it went under the hammer. Monstrous. He can't do that sort of thing."

"That's not so serious, is it?"

"Not serious? Of course it is. Virtually prostitution, that's what it is. Selling your opinion for money while pretending to be motivated only by the wish to find out the truth? Besides, what reputation would the committee have if everyone thought its opinions were swayed by how much the owners were willing to hand over? Disgraceful."

He seemed really shocked, which Flavia thought a bit excessive, considering how he made his own living.

"That's not the same at all," he said primly. "Everybody knows art dealers are in it for the money. That's why no one trusts us. Academics, paid by the state to be objective, are entirely different. They shouldn't take rake-offs.''

''Money,'' she said with satisfaction when his little burst of piety subsided. ''Always helpful to have a money motive in a murder case, so I'm told.''

''Not much, mind you. That picture might fetch a hundred and fifty thousand dollars on a good day. It's only a sketch. Five per cent of that is only seven and a half thousand. Not enough to kill anyone for, I reckon. Perhaps it was a threesome—the founder members, Bralle, Roberts and Kollmar.''

''And Masterson?''

''Kollmar discovers she has gone to Milan, where she would find out about his suppression of evidence.''

''How?''

''How what?''

''How does he discover she has gone to Milan?''

Argyll waved his hand airily to dismiss such trivialities. ''How should I know. I am hypothesising. Facts are your business. Anyway, he slips away at the opera, knifes her, and slips back. Or Roberts does.''

''And who pinches the pictures? Signora Pianta?'' She glanced at him sceptically. ''You make it sound more like a game of musical chairs than a murder investigation.''

Argyll was stumped, which was a pity as he had been starting to enjoy himself. ''Oh, well, I've no doubt the explanation will come to me in due course.''

It was a long drive; much too long for consistent conversation and, besides, they were already tired by the time they started. After stopping for dinner it was nearly midnight before they even got to the French border. Once they'd crossed, Argyll, who had taken over the driving and was proceeding at a more genteel pace, pulled the car off the road.

"What's up?" she asked as he cut the engine.

"Sleep. I'm exhausted. We've still got a long way to go and even if we kept driving we'd arrive at five in the morning, which is too early. So I'm going to have a nap."

It was a sensible decision, so she let back the car seat, wrapped her mother's coat around her and took his advice. They were fairly high up in the mountains and the air outside was cold, Argyll noticed as the car cooled down. He began to shiver. Why on earth could they not have gone to a hotel? He was not, he decided, going to spend the entire night listening to his teeth chattering. He slipped as gently as possible underneath the coat as well.

"What you doing?" she murmured, half-consciously.

"Basic survival technique," he replied, starting slightly as the brake lever dug into his back. "Body warmth. Good-night."

They stayed like that for perhaps four hours, sleeping remarkably well considering that Alfa Romeos are not really designed for such purposes. Then the dawn chorus and Flavia's coffee cravings woke them and they drove on to find a café for breakfast.

From there on, the journey was a quiet one. The traffic was as light as expected for a Saturday morning and the conversation was a little muted. Sharing the driving meant they spent about another five hours on the trip and both were stiff and tired when, shortly after lunch, Flavia spotted a small painted sign, half covered with overgrowth, that informed passers-by that Balazuc, *Village Historique*, lay a mere 3.8 kms down a narrow track to their left. "Thank God for that," Flavia said as Argyll, now driving once again, headed down it.

"What do we do when we get there?" he asked. "Georges Bralle, Balazuc, is not the most precise of addresses."

"Find the bar, I suppose," she replied, folding the map and peering out at the rocky hills on either side. She looked a bit surprised by the rough scenery, but as she had not taken her nose out of the map book for a couple of hours she had not had much chance to accustom herself to the changing landscape.

"Rather pretty, isn't it?" he said as he guided the car up the narrow and winding road into the gorge. "Good heavens."

The village appeared suddenly as they rounded a bend, looking as though it had grown out of the rocks of the steep cliff wall that fell directly into the river. It was an extraordinary sight, with scarcely a building to be seen that was not medieval.

"Most impressive," she said generously. "Almost as good as Tuscany."

The major disadvantage of the village, whatever its physical attractions, however, was that the one bar it possessed was closed. Nor was it exactly a hive of activity. There was one street, innumerable little alleyways too narrow to drive down and not a person to be seen in any of them.

"I don't think anyone has lived here since the Middle Ages," Argyll commented. "What should we do, shout and see what happens?"

They looked over a parapet and down the gorge while Flavia considered. Then she walked over to the nearest house and pressed the doorbell. No one replied. There was no one in the next house either, or the next.

"Looks as though they've all been converted into holiday houses. Bit of a problem, eh?" she observed. "There must be someone here, somewhere."

A quiet buzzing sound came to them from the other side of the valley and, presently around the corner, about a mile away, they saw a small yellow van. Argyll squinted at it. "A postman," he said with relief. "And heading our way. All our troubles may soon be over."

With great attention, they watched the little van curl its way along the road, over the bridge, stop and pick up some mail, go another hundred yards and stop again. Then it disappeared from sight before eventually reappearing. It slowed down as it passed their Milan-registered car, and the driver perused this strange apparition. Evidently a novelty round here. Argyll waved him down and a lengthy conversation ensued. It ended with Argyll pointing in one direction, the postman shaking his head and pointing in the other, then reaching down and handing over a packet of envelopes. Argyll came back.

"What was all that about?"

"Apparently it's a bit complicated. We'll have to walk, and the postman asked me if I wouldn't mind delivering the letters for all the houses up there, if I was going in that direction."

"But is Bralle there?"

"He didn't know. He hasn't seen him for ten days or more. But he gave the impression that's not unusual. Come on."

The little alley they took led them out of the top of the village into open countryside. The view was breathtaking, and Flavia's breath was duly taken, although that was more due to the incline and her lack of regular exercise than the panoramic beauty of the scene.

"He'd better be in after all this," she said grumpily. "Are you sure this is the right route?"

Argyll nodded in order to keep signs of his equally breathless state to himself. "Must be one of those," he said as they reached the top of the hill and saw a couple of houses in the distance, both perched on the cliff edge.

It wasn't the first, as that had the wrong name on the gate. Argyll dropped some of his envelopes into the box and they walked on. The gate of the second house announced in small brass letters that Georges Bralle lived here.

Some of the time, perhaps, but it didn't look as though he did at the moment. The thickly-built stone house was shuttered up, and there was no sign of life at all from the outside.

"Oh, dear. I think we may have had a long and tiring voyage for nothing."

Flavia grunted in disappointment. "Better go and make sure, I suppose. Damn the man. Why on earth can he not have a telephone?"

They knocked hopefully and heavily on the door, without much expectation of getting anyone to answer. Nobody did. They walked around and banged on the shutters. Nothing again. Argyll looked disgruntled, Flavia as though she was about to cry.

"Don't worry," he said comfortingly. "Maybe he's gone for a morning constitutional."

"After lunch? With the windows shuttered up? No chance. He's not here."

She sat down on a stone in the driveway to be fed up in comfort, so Argyll wandered off on his own for a last chance examination for signs of life. Not all the windows were shuttered, he noted. One small opening—a bathroom, maybe—had none. He peered at it, a worrying idea coming into his head. Don't you dare, he thought. On the other hand, Flavia was feeling miserable and, what was worse, could well decide to sit there the entire day, just in case Bralle turned up.

Without considering the matter further, he searched for footholds and handholds and levered himself up. And up. And when he was nearing the window, he glanced around and realised what he was doing. If he dropped off, he would not only fall fifteen or so feet down to stony and irregular ground, he would probably bounce off the narrow ledge into the gorge below. He paused and considered. It was probably more dangerous to go back down than to go ahead, so he inched his way further, wondering what he was to do when he reached his destination.

The window was fastened, but fitted its frame so badly it hardly required an expert burglar—which Argyll surely wasn't—to force it open without damage. He eased himself forward through the opening, got half-way, realised there was no way of turning round, panicked, over-balanced and toppled head first into a bidet. This was followed by a prolonged silence while he eased himself complainingly off the floor and made sure all bones were still in the right place and of the requisite length.

"Monsieur Bralle?" he called, just in case the old man was sleeping and had been woken up by the intrusion. "Hello?"

No reply, so he cautiously opened the bathroom door and ventured out into the corridor. Not a sound. It was an old man's house, no doubt about that, with the odd, musty, decayed smell that they often have. He flicked on a light switch, and the light came on. A good sign, surely. If anyone had gone away for a long period they would have cut it off at the mains. He located the staircase, and went down.

A hallway, with doors on either side. He opened the one to the left, which led into a dining-room with a kitchen just visible beyond. Neither had any sign of life. Then into the next room, a sitting-room, again empty but with a much stronger smell. Beyond that was another door, which led to a study and which contained the source of the now sickly odour.

"Yuch," he said in horror. Georges Bralle—or at least, he was willing to assume it was he and was not overdisposed to check on minor details—sat in a chair. He was slumped over the desk, and had evidently not moved for some time. He was, to put it another way, dead and rapidly going off.

It wasn't the shock of coming suddenly and unexpectedly across a dead man, although Argyll had little enough experience of this sort of thing; nor was it particularly the thought that the death might have been violent in some as yet undetermined fashion. Rather it was the distinctly shiny green tinge to him, the overpowering smell and the large, overnourished bluebottle buzzing lazily around that made Argyll take two steps back, swing round and deposit what remained of breakfast in the corner of the room with a violent and overpowering upsurge of nausea.

The effort exhausted him, and he sat himself on the sofa to recover, hardly daring to look at Bralle. His dominant feeling was now one of considerable embarrassment, although, thinking as rationally as possible, he considered that throwing up was an entirely natural reaction in the circumstances. Anybody would do the same, he told himself as he staggered off to where he remembered the toilet was located.

That finished, and deciding he had already done enough damage to whatever evidence the house might contain, he went to the front door to find Flavia. It was locked, but not bolted, and there was no key. The back door was both locked and bolted. He thought about that, then opened the main window of the dining-room, unfastened the shutters, and climbed out.

Flavia, still sitting on her stone and contemplating the iniquities of life, was surprised to see him emerge from the building, and even more concerned when she noticed his very pallid complexion.

"Bralle's in there," he said as he approached. "He's dead."

"Another one?" she said with some surprise but still taking the news a bit more calmly than he had done. "Killed, or natural causes? He was nearly eighty, after all."

"Where are you going?"

"To see for myself," she replied as she marched off to the window.

"I don't think that's a very good idea," he protested as he chased after her, half worrying that she would be upset by Bralle, but equally concerned to conceal the evidence of his own reaction. "You said you didn't like dead bodies."

There was no dissuading her. "God, what a smell. Where is he?"

Argyll led her through into the study. Flavia wrinkled her nose up in disgust, observed carefully and turned pale. But her digestive system, as usual, was made of stronger stuff than Argyll's.

"I know how you feel," he said supportively as they left the building. "What do we do now?"

There were, she decided, two, or rather three, things to be done. Argyll would go back to the village and call the police. Then he was to telephone Pierre Janet, Bottando's Parisian *alter ego*, and tell him what was going on. For her part, she would stay and do a little investigating. But first she sat on a stone outside the house to recover.

"You feeling all right?" Argyll asked before he headed off.

She shook her head silently, then stood up, and burst into tears, her body shaking with heavy, mournful sobs. For days she had been battling with this case, and every time she seemed to be making progress, it slipped away. Finding a new body every couple of days merely emphasised her confusion and made her realise how unpleasant her task really was. The effort to keep collected and professional finally proved too much.

"Oh, my dear Flavia," Argyll said, taken completely by surprise. He put his arms around her and squeezed reassuringly. She clung on to him tightly.

"Sometimes," she said breathlessly between sobs, "I think I'm not very good at this. I'm not sure I'm cut out for it."

Argyll rocked her from side to side and stroked her hair, saying nothing at all but feeling deeply moved. He was used to her rages, but was absolutely unprepared for this side of her. "Perhaps. But you're better at it than I am. At least you weren't sick."

She laughed and snuffled and sobbed some more.

"We could just go home afterwards and forget it, if you like," he added.

She let go of him and then extracted a tiny handkerchief from her pocket, blew the last trump into it, and sniffed loudly. Then shook her head fervently. "No. Off you go. I'm sorry. I shall just grit my teeth and get on with it."

She watched as he disappeared down the hill and then,

with immense reluctance and still feeling shaky, forced herself to go back into the house. It was the very last thing she wanted to do and, besides, she knew it was both unprofessional and discourteous. As an Italian, she had no right to look at, or touch, anything concerning a murder of a Frenchman that had taken place on French soil. Assuming it was a murder, of course.

Which was, of course, the problem. The French would probably sit on all the evidence and would fail to recognise anything significant even if it was there. Ordinarily this would be fine; the information would come through Janet eventually. But she was mindful of the omnipresent budget submission and aware that the clock was ticking. Bottando wanted a solution and her continued employment depended on it. The only sensible option was to have a quick sniff around before the locals went all territorial on her.

Sniff, alas, was too appropriate a word. She reckoned she'd have about forty minutes before the police turned up, but only ten or so before she felt overwhelmingly sick. Steeling herself, and moving very carefully so as not to disturb or leave any prints, she began the distasteful business of searching Bralle's desk. It was full of papers, but contained nothing she was interested in, except for a letter thanking Jones College, Massachusetts for the invitation to write a reference for James Miller but declining on the grounds of his retirement. It recommended Masterson instead. They knew that already, of course. But on second thoughts, she folded it up and tucked it in her bag. Just in case.

On the floor, underneath the desk, was a diary that was a more profitable read. A spidery, old man's hand had written in the space for October 3, ''St Gall.'' They knew that as well; but it was nice to have confirmation. What remained to be established was what he and Masterson had been doing there.

Most of the diary was blank. Evidently Bralle led a quiet life. But, four days after the first entry was the notation "St Anthony." What a busy little saint he was. Crops up everywhere in this case, she thought.

She put the diary down and examined the rest of the room. All along one wall was a bank of green metal filing cabinets which, when opened, seemed to contain the old man's life work of notes and writings. There was an awful lot of it. But then, if you spent sixty years doing little but writing away, there would be a hefty amount. She glanced into the first drawer. Dozens upon dozens of green files, all neatly arranged and organised, with little white tags at the top saying what, supposedly, they contained. She ran her fingers along them; nearly all files on paintings and painters of the Italian Renaissance.

She went through the papers methodically. There was no time to look through the contents, of course, but at least she could glance over the titles. It was a waste of time. Even his correspondence files seemed deadly dull and unproductive. But she at least fished out the originals of the documentation that Bralle had given to Benedetti. Bit naughty, but Argyll might find it useful.

By now she'd had more than enough. The smell was making her feel really ill and, although bearable if her searches were producing anything, it was insupportable otherwise. She climbed back out of the window, took deep breaths of clear fresh country air to clean out the passages, and waited for Argyll to return.

When he eventually puffed and blew his way back up the hill, he said he'd phoned Janet first and he, sweet old soul that he was, had said he would inform Bottando. He had also suggested Flavia might tell the locals that he had given her permission to talk to Bralle. Otherwise they might get stroppy and petulant about her presence. She was to phone him later and he would come down if necessary. The local police, meanwhile, were on the way.

They were, and made the next few hours miserable. While awfully excited about the prospect of a real murder at last on their turf, they were less enthusiastic when they viewed the physical evidence for themselves. One officer had the same initial reaction as Argyll, but apart from that, they did little to win the sympathy of their visitors, especially when they said they could find no evidence of the old man's death being anything other than natural causes. It was only when Flavia threw a fit and threatened to phone Janet once more that they grudgingly consented to order a post-mortem. In revenge, they were distinctly unfriendly about the Italian's presence in France.

Doctors came and went, the body was carted away in an ambulance, photographers and all the other official-dom of death bustled about, keeping their opinions firmly to themselves. Apart from having to give their own fin-gerprints, Argyll and Flavia were ignored and eventually it was made clear that their presence was not at all welcome.

Flavia, who hadn't really expected anything better, accepted the situation with patience and took her revenge by telling them as little as she could about her own case. They weren't going to help her, she wasn't going to help them.

"How nice it is," Argyll observed as they trudged back down the hill after their dismissal, "to see inter-national co-operation working so smoothly."

Flavia snorted. "Get me back to Venice," she said.

CHAPTER

12

By the time they arrived, horribly early, on Sunday morning, Bottando was back from Rome. He was not happy. This emotional state he manifested through a series of elliptical references to the need for discipline in police-work and disapproving comments on people who went off on holidays with their boyfriends in the middle of a case. Flavia apologised humbly for having omitted to inform him of their little diversion via the South of France, and did point out that at least they had discovered another death. Besides, she added, Argyll was not her boyfriend.

"But you're not meant to be finding more," he said grumpily. "You're meant to be dealing with the more than adequate supply we have already. Still," he continued reluctantly, "it was quite good work, I suppose. The trouble is, it has sent the men in suits in Rome into a renewed frenzy. They want results and the department is now being held responsible. We get the flak if we don't come up with a solution, not Bovolo."

"Does that mean the Masterson business has been officially reopened?"

"Oh, no. Nothing so simple," he said bitterly. "They merely want a clearing-up operation, reconciling all the pieces. I tried to point out that what we know cannot be reconciled with Bovolo's conclusions, but that made very little impression. That, I think, is the point. Not sorting this out demonstrates our incompetence and strengthens the hand of the people who want to carve us up."

Now Flavia understood his pique better. But there was nothing she could do or say to cheer him up, so she asked if he had spoken to Janet.

"Oh, yes. That's why I'm here. At least he's reliable. More so than the local police in the Ardèche, I must say."

"Nothing of any help?"

"Just that it was definitely murder."

"We know that."

"How come so sure?"

"Because," she explained, "Jonathan here noticed that all the doors were locked and there were no keys on the inside."

Argyll looked becomingly modest.

"I see," Bottando said. "Ah, well, it's good to have official confirmation too, I suppose. In case you hadn't noticed this as well, it was suffocation. Pillow over the face. Bits of fluff up his nose, or something. I doubt they would have even given him a postmortem in more normal circumstances, he was so old. Had a wonky heart anyway, it seems. But your insistence and a timely intervention from friend Janet made them a bit more conscientious, fortunately.

"Apart from that, not much. No fingerprints, no witnesses, no nothing, as seems to be usual in this case. Nothing missing, nothing untoward at all. Killed on Oc-

tober 7th, give or take a day. Isn't precision wonderful?''
he finished sarcastically.

"St Anthony strikes again," she said, a little too cryp-
tically for Bottando's delicate state. He asked her what
she meant.

"In Bralle's diary there is an entry for October 7th
which said merely 'St Anthony.' I suppose he was doing
something about that picture then.''

"Or the saint himself descended from heaven, suffocated him and rose to the skies once more. Divine intervention. A miracle. How about that?'' Argyll suggested
helpfully.

"Tempting, but it wouldn't look good in an official
police report," Bottando replied impatiently.

"Well, at least we've made some progress," Flavia
said hopefully.

"I'm glad you think so. I'm not so sure. But you really
shouldn't break into houses on foreign territory, purloin
evidence, or vanish without saying where you're going.
Just as well I'm here to remember what policework is
really all about.''

"So tell us what we should be doing.''

"Emulate me. I have been methodically going over the
evidence in accordance with established police procedure,'' he said pompously.

"And getting nowhere as usual, I suppose?''

He looked offended. "Well, since you mention it, no.
What have you done?''

"What we, in our amateurish way have discovered, is
this," she said in a superior fashion. "Firstly, the picture
in Milan is so genuine Jonathan here is going to buy it.''

"Oh, God. It'll be stolen within a week.''

"Control yourself," she said primly. "Things aren't
as bad as that. Secondly, Masterson, Roberts, Kollmar

and Bralle all knew it, but all except Masterson seemed
concerned not to let on. Masterson met Bralle in St Gall
just before she came to Venice. Next, his diary suggested
he was involved with her work on the St Anthony cycle
of pictures in Padua.''

Bottando was grudgingly impressed, but determined
not to show it. ''Is that all?''

''Then there's the case of the authentication,'' Flavia
said, with a brief explanation of Roberts' offer to Benedetti.

''Ah, I do wish you'd make up your minds,'' Bottando
said wearily, leaning back in his seat and stretching.
''From having no motives at all, we now seem to be
swimming in them. How very tiresome. Well, I suppose
we will now have to do some more work. It seems this
is a case of one murder leading to another. Find who
killed Bralle and presumably you find who rubbed out
all the rest of them. And everything else will fall into
place. We'll have to go round these infernal people once
again. Goodness, but I'm getting sick of this case.''

''Before you run off,'' Argyll put in, ''is there, by any
chance, any progress on my pictures, now that self-
portrait may be worth having?''

''No. Nothing at all. I know where they all are, of
course, but that's different.''

Argyll seemed astonished and hopeful all at the same
time. ''You know? Where are they?''

Bottando smirked. ''In the obvious place. Come on,''
he said, standing up slowly. ''To work.''

The strain of being involved in a murder investigation
was beginning to tell on the various members of the committee who still survived. Initially, they had nearly all
been somewhat supercilious about the questioning and,

with the exception of Van Heteren, had seemed little moved by Masterson's death. But now that Death the Reaper was going on a major recruiting drive, so to speak, with especial emphasis on art historians, their nervousness was increasing quite markedly.

The bulky Van Heteren came first, wedged into the tiny armchair in his grubby rooms and no more pleased with life than he had been earlier in the week. If anything, he looked worse. That was sad; he was the only one for whom Flavia felt any rapport at all and Bottando, now meeting all of these characters for the first time, saw why.

He had decided to do the interviewing himself, to see if a fresh perspective added anything to what they knew already. It was not that he did not trust Flavia; far from it. She would have to be there to help out with the languages when he saw Miller, but Kollmar and Van Heteren he could manage on his own while she went off to examine other angles.

"I thought the investigations were all over," Van Heteren said after he had arrived. Both were portly men, and in the tiny apartment almost had to wedge themselves side by side to fit in. "So why are we being kept here? I have to vacate this place by Monday at the latest."

"Is your timetable so very important?"

He looked at him sharply, then grinned half-heartedly. "Selfish of me, right? I suppose it is. My apologies. Thinking about work in the circumstances is pitiful. But I'm coming to hate this place, and I have my doubts that you'll ever find who killed Louise."

"There are things to be dealt with," he pointed out. "Bralle, for example." He explained about the man's death. Van Heteren was thoroughly shocked by the news.

"Surely you can't think that one of us killed poor old Georges?"

"Someone killed poor old Georges. So why not one of you? Where were you, by the way, when he was killed?"

Very reluctantly, he said he was on a walking tour in the Alps. A late holiday. Yes, on his own. No, he couldn't prove he did not go to Balazuc. But no, he hadn't.

"I see. Pity. And on the night that Roberts died, and those paintings were stolen?"

He was in his room. On his own. He'd been too depressed and miserable after Louise had been killed to do anything or see anyone. No alibi, in other words.

"Ah, ha," he said as neutrally as possible. "You seem to me to be a very worried man, doctor."

"Is that any surprise?" he replied acidly. "My best friend and lover murdered, two colleagues dying and the obvious suspicion that you think one of us is responsible. Which, I imagine, we are. I don't know how high up your list of suspects I am, but I can assure you that never, whatever she might have done, would I ever have harmed Louise. Do you believe me?"

Bottando shrugged noncommittedly. "Be reasonable," he said. "You would hardly say anything else. But, if it makes you feel any better, I do not think you killed her. Satisfied?"

He nodded, scarcely reassured, so Bottando continued. "Did you know Masterson was interested in a picture owned by the Marchesa di Mulino?"

Vaguely, he said. He'd been talking to her at the party Lorenzo had thrown the year before. It was when they were most deeply involved, so he'd thought. She'd playfully pointed out a picture, a portrait, and asked him what he thought of it. He'd said that it seemed without any merit at all and she'd laughed.

"And?" Bottando prompted.

"And nothing. That was all. We were a little drunk by then. It was a good party. Lorenzo knows how to throw them. Food, music, lots to drink, beautiful surroundings. She spent a long time looking at it and then gave the slightly swaying view that it was an interesting face, didn't I think? Not a nice man, but an interesting one. I said that was a very scholarly assessment. Then she said it needed work."

"What did she mean?"

"I assume that it needed a lot of cleaning and restoration. It was very dirty and unkempt. Anyway, then she giggled and suggested going back to her room to celebrate her powers of discernment. So we did. She was in a really good mood, probably the happiest I'd ever seen her," he said, remembering the event with obvious pain.

"You mentioned to my assistant that Masterson was going to write a reference for Dr Miller?"

He nodded.

"Did she mention this to anyone else, do you know?"

"I'm sure she didn't. I only knew because I saw a draft of it on her desk. In fact she told me specifically not to mention it; said she supposed she would have to write a good reference, but she was damned if she saw why anyone had to know about it. She didn't want to take the blame for someone as boring as him getting tenure. I think she should have said what she thought, but she was much too soft to do that."

Bottando nodded sagely. Had Masterson mentioned meeting Bralle in Switzerland? Discussed her trip to Milan? To Padua? The answers to all were that she had not. He had no idea she had travelled so much in her last few days. Not, perhaps, that it was surprising. She always was busy. That was the trouble.

• • •

James Miller was also quickly disposed of, although he
also contributed little of obvious material use. His hair
was wet and he rubbed it down with a towel as he explained that he had just got back from a swim. He swam
every day, he said.

Bottando looked carefully around his room, making
halting, Anglo-Italian conversation until Flavia turned up,
looking pleased with herself. Miller's Italian was remarkably bad for someone who had spent so many years
working on things Italian. Clearly it was not he who had
spoken to Pianta the day of Masterson's murder.

He asked how long Miller was planning to stay in Venice and was told the American was desperate to get back
home as quickly as possible. He was already late and the
events of the past week would not do his forthcoming
battle for tenure any good at all. He sounded almost half-
crazed with anxiety, and failed very dismally in his attempts to seem light-hearted about it. Flavia brought up
the question of his reference. She seemed interested in it.
He replied gruffly that he could imagine what Masterson
would have said.

"How?" she asked.

"Well, we had a bit of a disagreement on Thursday. I
suppose you ought to know that. I said I hoped she was
going to go easy on poor old Kollmar. I was trying to
give her the benefit of my experience. Antagonising people is not the best way of getting what you want."

"And she didn't like it?" She could imagine the scene;
Miller slipping into condescension as he instructed her,
Masterson bristling. She did not seem the sort of person
who would take kindly to such advice.

"Evidently not, considering how snappishly she turned
down his offer of a drink the next day. In fact, she blew

a fuse and said she was sick to death of everybody making mountains out of molehills and wished people wouldn't be so goddamned hypersensitive. And in my case, I would be much better if I spent more time doing my own work and spent less time on academic arse-licking.''

"Meaning?"

"Tenure again. She reckoned that I hadn't written enough."

"And have you?"

He shook his head. "Don't think the *Encyclopedia Britannica* would be long enough to satisfy Louise. But, as I told her, I am about to produce a major article. I gave her a copy of it.

"Funny, isn't it?" he commented with a bitterness that was almost embarrassing in its self-centredness. "I joined this committee because I thought it would help my career. Now, at the crucial moment, all hell breaks loose. The committee is involved in scandal and I lose both of my referees. Louise was bad enough, although it's difficult to imagine she would have been generous on my behalf. But Roberts dying as well is just too horrible. I can't believe anyone else will be queuing up to offer their services now, can you? The mortality rate is too high."

Then Bottando chipped in, to get the conversation on to more immediate concerns. Time was short. Miller produced his passport and airplane ticket to prove that he was in Greece when Georges Bralle died, and said he had not seen the old man for nearly three years. His alibis for the nights Masterson and Roberts died were equally consistent and still solid.

"Well?" asked Bottando as they headed back to the exit. "Any luck?"

"I think so," she said. "The water from the leak

stopped about there.'' She went on, pointing back down
the corridor. ''I spoke to the keeper of the building. Nothing wrong with the roof at all. More importantly, he
pointed out what I should have remembered myself, that
it rained for the first time in three weeks when I went
boating with Jonathan a couple of days ago.''

Bottando smiled back. ''Do you know,'' he said as
they walked to the vaporetto stop, ''I am just beginning
to think that, with a bit of luck, we might keep our jobs
after all.''

Dr Kollmar was equally displeased to see him, but Bottando was getting used to it by now. While the German
had been ill at ease when he'd met Flavia, now he was
vibrating visibly as he came in and sat down.

''I suppose you think I killed her because of that picture,'' he said in a gloomy but ill-natured mood which
scarcely helped to enlist Bottando's sympathies.

''The thought had occurred,'' he said. ''Did you?''

''Of course I didn't,'' he replied with more spirit than
usual. ''What an absurd idea.''

''I've read your report. Roberts thought the picture was
genuine, there was evidence to prove it and you disre-
garded both. Why?''

He seemed genuinely astonished. ''What?'' he asked.
''You're completely wrong on both counts. Professor
Roberts never said anything of the sort, and the evidence
I found in my searches through the archives produced
nothing conclusive at all.''

''And what about other people's searches? Like Dr
Bralle's?''

''I don't know what you're talking about,'' he said
stiffly. ''Bralle was retired and if he had any views on
that picture he never told me. I suggest you confine your-

self to policework and stop trying to tell me how to do my—"

"How much was your cut, doctor?" Bottando asked dryly.

He looked puzzled again. "I beg your pardon?"

"Your cut. You know."

There was a long pause, then Kollmar said stiffly, "If you are suggesting what I think, then I must tell you that is outrageous and disgraceful. How dare you even think that—"

"Yes, yes. Right. Sorry I mentioned it," he said. "But did you really believe that picture was a fake?"

He mangled his hands in minor anguish, then sighed. "There was considerable doubt . . ."

"So why didn't you say so?"

"Because I thought it safer to follow Professor Roberts' advice. In the absence of documentary evidence everything depends on stylistic assessment. That was his area, not mine."

He was sitting, primly and upright, knees together in his chair and consumed by what passed for considerable anger. All signs of his early nervousness had vanished during the questioning. Bottando sighed, and tried to ease the man back into a more cooperative spirit. He didn't do very well.

"The Fenice," he began. Kollmar groaned wearily.

"How often do I have to tell you people about that. I went to the opera. I sat with Roberts and my wife throughout."

"One part of your alibi is dead, the other is related. Not good, doctor."

He kept a dignified silence.

"OK, then. The night Roberts died. Where were you?"

"I've told you several times already. I delivered an

envelope to his house then went home. I fed the children
and tried to get on with some work.''

''Alone?''

''Yes, alone.''

''I see. One last question. When you asked Masterson
for a drink, was it on the island or on the boat leaving
it?''

''On the boat. You can ask Miller, he heard it all.''

''Thank you, doctor. That will do for today.''

He had endured enough for one morning. His head
hurt, and facts and theories were jumbled up inside it,
almost meeting but not quite there. Bottando made his
way out of the dismal house into the even more dismal
street outside. It was raining hard now, as the old boatman had assured Flavia it would. He looked at the grey
overcast sky, and wrapped himself up more firmly for
protection against the bitter wind blowing in strongly
from the lagoon, and hurried at a brisk trot towards the
quayside. He was late and talking to Kollmar had cut
into his lunch. He'd have to skip food entirely if he
wanted to get to his meeting with Bovolo on time. Dam-
nation. If there was one thing Bottando resented, it was
missing lunch.

Argyll was equally busy all morning, invigorated by the
prospect of recovering his pictures. He had rung up
Byrnes in London to ask him to sniff around for Titians
on the market in the last few years. How many were sold
with shiny new certificates of attribution? he wanted to
know, adding news of his own little venture into the same
line of business. Byrnes, somewhat mollified by the prospect of Argyll at last earning his salary, agreed to make
discreet enquiries and ring back.

Since then, he had left policework to the police, and

dedicated himself to tracking down the author of the Marchesa's painting. It might, after all, have a bearing on Masterson's murder and besides, Bottando seemed confident he could lay his hands on it. As Argyll could well own it soon, he thought it might be interesting to know what he was buying.

Knowing what you are looking for, however, is not the same as finding it, and in this department he made little progress. He had, variously, purloined notes off Masterson, had picked up her photocopies from the library and temporarily confiscated her books from the shelves. Taken together, he hoped that something appropriately convincing would emerge, but was forced to admit that there was, as yet, not even the hint of an answer in sight. Giorgione, Titian, and the none too appealing Pietro Luzzi. Clearly the little trio fitted together somehow, and equally obviously Masterson knew how. He was coming to the conclusion that she was a good deal cleverer than he was.

"So what do you know?" Flavia asked when she joined him for the lunch Bottando was being forced to miss.

He sniffed moodily. "Well, not much, really. I know that the portrait is of a painter in his thirties and that Titian painted him into his series in Padua and that sketch in Milan. That's about it."

"OK, then," Flavia said, trying to help. "Find out who all Titian's mates are and you're there. After all, painting friends into religious pictures was common enough. You mentioned that Titian stuck in his dead mistress, so why not others as well?'

Argyll looked at her. "Say that again," he said.

Flavia complied. "I said, you told me . . ."

"I was speaking purely rhetorically," he said briskly,

standing up and brushing the crumbs off his clothes. "Although it is good to hear it again. Oh, stupid, stupid, stupid."

"I hope you're referring to yourself?"

"Of course. It's obvious. Mistress, ha! I am, perhaps, the most dimwitted person you have ever known."

Flavia was often inclined to agree, but pretended on this occasion that she hadn't heard. "What are you talking about?"

He was leaping up and down and positively bubbling with enthusiasm. "Picture of Violante di Modena being murdered by her lover because she was unfaithful. Who else was her lover, apart, perhaps, from Titian? And who, therefore, painted that portrait of the Marchesa's? And why was Masterson so keen on it?"

"Oh, my God," she said, realisation dawning. "Come back here. I want to talk about this."

"No time," he burbled happily. "Work to be done." He bent over and kissed her on the forehead and then, in case that was a bit familiar in public, patted her head to make up for it.

"To work. You are a wonderful person, and perfectly wasted in the police. My thanks. See you later."

Having provided inspiration for Argyll, Flavia finished her lunch and forced herself out into the ever-deteriorating weather and off in the direction of Lorenzo. The problem, as she saw it, was a fairly simple one. They knew what had happened. The difficult bit now was tying the whole process together to make sense of it. One murder after another, presumably following a logical pattern, once you understood it. It was, after all, a serious business, killing people. Not to be undertaken without a very good reason.

"Oh, yes, I knew my aunt was going to sell some pictures," Lorenzo replied after she'd arrived at his apartment, had been let in, had dried herself off and sat down. "But I wasn't too sure which ones. My only concern was that she didn't sell a couple of Watteau drawings I have always been most fond of. She said these were not the ones, and so I took very little extra interest in it and gave my permission."

"And they're not valuable, you're sure of that?"

"Oh, no. Very minor stuff. No danger of a Michelangelo slipping unnoticed out of the country, rest assured of that."

He looked perfectly at ease and she decided not to make him dissatisfied about his decision. "How do you get on with your aunt?"

"Not very well. We tolerate each other, as aunt and nephew have to do. I rather like the old bat, I must admit. She, alas, doesn't like me much."

"Why not?"

"I really don't know. She doesn't like having to consult me over financial matters, of course. It dents her self-image as head of the family and she was furious when she found out how my uncle had set up his will in my favour. I think I'm absolutely charming, and I always try hard to please, but she seems to think I'm too frivolous. A playboy. She's fond of out-dated slang. Lord only knows what she thinks I get up to. I'm fairly certain my life is not half as scandalous as hers was."

If there was any great animosity, he hid it well and appeared to be affectionately tolerant of the old lady, rather than resenting her. "And how about Signora Pianta?"

He rolled his eyes. "Echt. The dragon lady. I've known her ever since she moved in on my aunt some quarter century ago. She came to stay for a week, and is still there. But she's a poor thing, literally and figuratively, and I'm always as civil as I can be to her.''

''And where were you on the night that Roberts died and your aunt's pictures were stolen?'' Worth a chance; he might always contradict himself.

He smiled happily. ''Not going to get me there,'' he said ''I was at a meeting at the Accademia. At the time in question I was delivering a short, but if I may say so, tolerably amusing, speech to about a hundred and fifty people.'' He added, ''I'll give you the museum's number. When they open up tomorrow morning they can give you the names of several dozen people able to confirm where I was until midnight.''

He said it with such confidence that Flavia knew his alibi would be unshakeable. Evidently, he had not rubbed out Roberts. Just time to heist the Marchesa's goodies, though, if he was quick about it, or got someone else to do it for him. What else? One last question. ''The party at your aunt's last year. What was it for?''

He shrugged with an expression of some surprise at the question, whose point he evidently missed. ''It was partly a welcome for Louise as the new member of the committee, and partly a joyous celebration of the opening of the state's coffers. The happy taxpayer was paying. And, of course, partly to establish myself in the eyes of my colleagues as the head of the committee.''

''Which, if I understand things correctly, did not go down at all well with Professor Roberts.''

Lorenzo smiled amiably once more. ''Dreadful thing to talk ill of the dead,'' he said, ''but you're right, of course. I don't mind saying that poor old Roberts was losing his touch. As for the party, it was a great success. So much so, I was going to give another last Saturday, complete with flowers from the Giardinetti greenhouses. Louise chose them. Particularly wanted lilies, I don't know why. She said it had something to do with her work.''

"Why do you think she was so convinced Kollmar was wrong about that Milan picture?" she went on, vaguely conscious of a series of half-forged connections waiting for a missing link.

"Still plugging away at that, are you? I don't know. What did she think it was?"

"A sketch for the third, abandoned panel of the St Anthony series in Padua," Flavia said.

"Ah. Most interesting. I confess I haven't looked all that carefully. I skipped the meeting; I had to be in Rome that day, and missing a report by Kollmar is never a great loss. A thorough and dedicated man, but not what you might call one of the most lively of scholars. As for Masterson, I assume she must have found evidence in the picture indicating the presence of St Anthony, something in the story-line, whatever it was, to pin it down to an episode in the saint's life—''

"It could be," she said, telling him about the relevant miracle.

"Not good enough," he said. "Saving people from poisoning or murder crops up time and again in the lives of the saints. What else was in the picture?"

Flavia thought hard, and wished she had a photograph on her to refresh her memory. Argyll always had better visual recall than she did. But she did her best. "Man eating at a table, surrounded by people. Angels buzzing about. Cross on the wall. Flowers on the table.''

"Lilies?"

Flavia glanced up and stared. A penny was on the brink of dropping. Clearly her unconscious was better at her job than she was. "Why do you say that?"

"Symbol of St Anthony," he replied simply. "Lilies and a crucifix. Bodily purity and love of God. Generally accompanied by the inscription, *'homo igit consutut atque nudat queso ubi est.'* Job. 'A man dies and he disappears, man comes to his end and where is he?' " He paused. "You seem surprised, but I'm sure I'm right. I can check, if you like."

"No," she said thoughtfully. "No, that's quite all right. You are right. Thank you. That is most helpful."

Bad news, or at least discomforting tidings, awaited her
when she got back to the Danieli at four. It took the form
of a discontented Bottando who was eating a late plate
of pasta with an air of profound melancholy. He waved
at her to sit down and said nothing until he had finished
it.

"Trouble," he said moodily before she could speak.
"That man Bovolo is beginning to get on my nerves."

He explained that his meeting with the Venetian had
not been much fun. Bovolo had launched into a denun-
ciation of interfering Romans and announced he had
taken strong measures—that was the term the silly man
had used, so Bottando assured his assistant—to stop his
position being undermined.

"What does that mean?"

"It means, my dear, that he doesn't like you. Or me,
for that matter. He thinks we have stuck our noses too
much into his murder investigation instead of confining
ourselves to tracking down the Marchesa's pictures. That
we are consorting with the main suspect—meaning Ar-

gyll—and that our—he means your—judgement is
highly compromised. That we have shown singular incompetence in wrapping up a simple theft when he has
solved a complicated murder in a matter of days. And he
has written strong letters to just about everybody damn-
ing us mightily. With the result that I have been fiercely
criticised by the polizia in Rome for my tactlessness, with
the Defence and Interior Ministries putting their penny-
worth in as well. We are not popular, and you know what
that means.''

''Oh, dear. What triggered this?''

''He's a worried man, that's why. He has cut far too
many corners and got the local investigating magistrate
to commit himself to saying Roberts was not murdered.
And we are trying to prove he was. If we succeed it will
make him look like a fool. The Marchesa is pressuring
him to take the guard out of her house. He wants this
whole thing shut down fast so he can take what credit is
going before everything turns sour on him and his promotion chances evaporate. And quite a lot of local dig-
nitaries are beginning to see his point of view.''

''So what do we do?''

Bottando rubbed his chin thoughtfully. ''Difficult, isn't
it? We find a murderer and we're in trouble. If we don't
find one, we're still in trouble. The problem is not Bovolo; I can take care of him. It's the local magistrate,
who's well-connected and influential. That's the trouble
spot. Split them apart, and we're OK. But if we suggest
the magistrate's office has connived in covering up Roberts' murder, then there'll be an unholy fight. We might
win, but not in time to save the department.

''Whatever happens, we've got to finish this stupid
investigation fast. Otherwise we might all be out of a job.
So, reassure me. Tell me it's all solved.''

"Sorry," she said sadly. "Can't do that. Nearly there, but there's a piece or two missing." She explained what Lorenzo had said about the lilies.

Bottando grunted. "But . . . ?"

"I know. Awkward, isn't it?"

Bottando grunted once more. "Well, that's another piece in place, anyway. The mystery of Roberts' dunking in the canal solved, at least."

"Indeed. Doesn't explain anything else, though."

Bottando sighed, and Flavia decided it would be a good idea to change the subject. "Have you seen Jonathan?"

Bottando checked his watch. "He should be here by now. He phoned to say he'd be over. But he's never been on time for anything before, so I see no reason why he should start now. Another similarity between you and him. How are you two getting on these days, hmm?"

She was spared having to make a tart comment about people minding their own business by the arrival of the subject of their discussion, in an unusually good humour.

"Hello, hello," he said brightly, as he sat down at their table. "What's wrong? Bad day?"

They told him, but news of their internal problems did little to lower his spirits. "It'll blow over," he said, dismissing their predicament airily. "Do you want to hear what I've found out?"

"As long as you're not going to tell us Roberts killed Masterson, yes."

This did dampen his mood. "Oh," he said. "Why do you say that?"

"Because he didn't."

"Are you sure?"

"Yes. Why?"

"Well, quite apart from efficiently doing my own

work, I also spent a long afternoon on the phone for your
benefit. You can thank me later. To Byrnes initially.
There have been five Titians for sale in the last decade.
And two authenticated by the committee after they were
sold. Both in the last four years.''

"So?"

"Want to guess where the owners lived?''

"No. Why don't you just tell us? It'll be quicker.''

"One lives in St Gall and the other in Padua. How
about that?''

He had their interest now, no doubt about that.

"My phone bill is enormous,'' he continued. "I hope
you are going to pay for it. I talked to both of them.
Neither met Masterson, but the Swiss man confirms he
talked to Bralle about the deal over the authentication.
Bralle disapproved mightily. In Padua Masterson delivered a letter from Bralle, again enquiring about the sale.
He's sending it on.

"Now, the point is,'' he went on enthusiastically,
"who wrote the reports on these pictures? And who is-
sued a personal authentication for them, in exchange for
a cut of the selling price which netted, in all, a total of
around two hundred and eighty thousand dollars?''

He handed over his notebook, in which he had made
a careful table of the committee's working methods and
distribution of work load alongside pictures examined
and authenticated.

Flavia's brain clanked over as piece after piece fell into
place, leading to conclusion after conclusion. Some were
annoying, because they were so obvious. Others were
distressing. Eventually she turned towards Bottando.
"General, I think we need to have a talk about this.''

"I think Mr Argyll has something else to tell us,''
Bottando said quietly.

"I do. Very important. About the Marchesa's picture."

"No time for that now. We can celebrate later. Unless it tells us more about the murderer. Does it?"

"Well, no. Not in this case."

"Then it'll have to wait. Jonathan, you go and ring this list of people," she scribbled on the back of a menu and handed him the list, "and tell them it is important they come to a meeting on the Isola San Giorgio. Say, nine o'clock."

"Is that a good idea? The water is awfully high. It's beginning to flood in some places already."

"No choice. We're running out of time," she replied briskly. Bottando studied her thoughtfully as she took control and started issuing orders. That was his role, he generally thought, but there was no denying she did it rather well. It was simply that he had a horrible idea he knew what was going through her mind. And she said *he* was a politician . . .

Argyll disappeared in the direction of the telephones with the list clutched tightly in his hand, and Flavia turned to her boss with a glint in her eye which convinced him he was correct.

"General," she began in her most persuasive of voices. "How do you feel about bending a rule or two? Not many, you realise. And just a little, to save the department?"

CHAPTER

14

Rain and wind had now firmly combined into a storm which, with the incoming tide, made the level of the water in the lagoon rise. With thick black clouds also hanging low in the sky over the city, Venice seemed very far from being a paradise for tourists; even the seagulls had vanished, evidently having gone elsewhere to sit it out and wait for calmer weather. On Saturday, the sea level had been higher than usual; on Sunday morning it was lapping near the top of the bank of the Piazza San Marco with particularly sharp gusts of wind blowing spray across the paving stones. By lunchtime the worst had happened and, despite the best attempts of the local authorities to deploy their limited stock of sandbags, the enemy was within. The optimists were fairly certain that Venice was not about to experience another trauma like 1966, when the entire place went several feet under, but damage was being done, of that there was no doubt.

Not only that, of course, but communications around the increasingly waterlogged city were becoming ever more difficult. The floating vaporetto stops, anchored to the sides of the canal by thick ropes, were rising with the water level. The boats were still running, although how much longer this would continue was uncertain. It was reaching the stops that was the trouble; improvised walkways were being laid on bricks and stones above the water, but the job was far from complete. Venice has a lot of streets and many of them were now below water level.

Getting round and staying moderately dry—comfort was out of the question—required thick shoes. Flavia had some, of course; she delved into her apparently bottomless suitcase and found a pair of stout, waterproof long boots that not only fitted, kept her dry but also looked good. Argyll had to make do with the heavy handstitched brogues that he seemed to have worn every day, in the deepest winter and the hottest summer, since Flavia had met him. They did the job better than expected, but the task would probably be their last before they had to be consigned to the rubbish pile.

Worst off was Bottando, who suffered most dreadfully from corns and who, as a result, wore soft leather Italian slip-on shoes which appeared to have soles made of cardboard. He kept the information about the corns to himself, generally believing that it was not an appropriate ailment for a man in his position, and had to put up with the occasional clever remark about his vanity as a result. As the shoes turned into mush on the way to the Isola San Giorgio and the fondazione Cini, he complained with some feeling about the state of the Italian shoe industry. It was not merely his feet making him uncomfortable, however. The whole business made him feel distressed.

The meeting had been called in some haste, but it seemed as though everyone had agreed to turn up. Bottando didn't like such scenes normally, but Flavia was right that speed was of the essence if he was to get back to Rome with the results before bureaucratic knives were plunged into his back on Monday morning.

"You should come better prepared," she told him as they sloshed along, implicitly congratulating herself on her foresight.

"You should buy better shoes to start off with," added Argyll, equally complacent about his own.

Bottando resisted the not very great temptation to reply to either of them and maintained a disgruntled silence as they got into the taxi-boat and made their way, slowly and with a great deal of turbulence, across the mouth of the Grand Canal.

"I just hope everybody gets there," he said pessimistically, glaring at the sky as though a sign of his displeasure might persuade it to mend its ways.

"They will," Flavia said. "After all, they have a certain interest in all this."

Silence again, as Bottando wiggled his toes around in what remained of his shoes—the fake gold-plated buckles were now the only bit of them still intact—and felt the salt water squishing around inside. He vowed never to come back to this awful place, and repeated the oath as they got out of the boat on the island. Not even planks here, he noticed as they waded their way across the jetty to the monastery entrance.

Inside, they briefly went their separate ways to find towels and dry themselves out as much as possible, then congregated in the room where the committee held its meetings. On the far side—no friendly conversation, Bottando noted—sat the Marchesa and Signora Pianta. The Marchesa watched them enter with amused interest and seemed blithely unconcerned about anything. She sat as though she owned the place.

Argyll looked keenly at the various people as they drifted in; he had not yet met any of them, and had built up images of them from Flavia's descriptions. She had done a good job, he reckoned, as he picked out the enormous Van Heteren with his air of depression and anxiety; the slightly pudgy, dapper Miller whose hunted expression suggested he was thinking of his job; the grey and dowdy Kollmar; the suavely elegant Lorenzo, who made a point of greeting his aunt with over-elaborate courtesy and was rewarded with a disdainful nod of acknowledgement and a nervous twitch from Pianta.

But no Bovolo. Where was the man? Bottando wondered as he cast his eyes around. He didn't want to start without him. He felt the steam beginning to rise from him in the stuffy, overheated room as he made his way to one of the seats left empty. Flavia sat down beside him and Argyll, fittingly doing his best to melt into the background, plonked himself down in a far corner.

"My thanks to you all for turning out on such an abominable night," Bottando began when he noticed everyone was sitting down and ready. They would have to do without Bovolo for a bit and hope he would turn up later. Initially he wanted Flavia to do the talking, as it was all her idea, but she had insisted that it would carry more weight coming from him. A little joke on her part. It showed she was feeling better. So she had explained the situation. Not in great detail, but enough to do the job quickly and get off to catch the last plane to Rome.

"I apologise for organising this set-piece discussion of the events of the last week or so, but I felt it would be for the good of everyone. All of you have come under suspicion, or have felt you have, in the course of this investigation. Clearly, in many cases this was erroneous. I am aware of the nature of academic life, and realise that the damage to your reputations through intemperate gossip could be considerable if the police do not give a clear account of proceedings so that the innocent are demonstrably cleared of all suggestion of, um, misbehaviour.''

Murmurings of gratitude for this official consideration, still tempered by a marked apprehension about what was to come. "All of you, for various reasons, deserve to know what has been going on, and it saves a great deal of our time to tell you all at once. We have already spent far too long on this case and have ended up investigating deaths which are not, and have never been, the responsibility of our department.'' A nod here in the direction of the magistrate, who looked mollified but still suspicious.

"You are not of course interested in our work schedule. As you are aware, this whole business began as an investigation into the murder of Louise Masterson, stabbed to death in the public garden by the Piazza San Marco last Friday night, and found in a greenhouse the following morning. Four days later her colleague on this committee, Professor Roberts, also died in mysterious circumstances, and the same evening a collection of paintings, belonging to the Marchesa di Mulino, disappeared. As we later discovered, the committee's founder, Georges Bralle, had been suffocated in his house in France some days before.

"Now, any idiot could see that this string of mortality and malfeasance was connected in some way with the committee's work.'' Perhaps it was just as well Bovolo was not there, although the magistrate was displeased once more. "The problem that had to be solved was which aspect of it.''

Bottando was beginning to enjoy himself. He paused

and looked around at the expressions on the people about him; ranging from acute pain on Van Heteren's and Miller's faces to the amused interest shown by the Marchesa.

"Far from being an agreeable collaboration of like-minded scholars, we discovered that the Titian committee was something of a hotbed of dislike and distrust. Georges Bralle had created the model of divide and rule, and eventually fell victim to it when Professor Roberts eased him out by arranging for a state grant he knew Bralle would find unacceptable. What Bralle began continued after his departure. For example, Masterson was widely expected to deliver a paper highly critical of Dr Kollmar, and Dr Lorenzo was tipped to use this as an excuse to replace him.

"When Louise Masterson arrived last year, she was seemingly anxious to create a good impression. That did not last long. On the second day she objected to Dr Kollmar's paper on a picture in Milan and said she wanted to re-examine it herself. She started to do just that. She wrote to Georges Bralle, making enquiries, and he said he didn't think Kollmar had made a mistake. Why did he say that, when he knew, from evidence he had himself provided, that Kollmar was wrong?

"This year, Masterson flies to Zurich, and takes a train to St Gall where Bralle is seeing someone who sold a Titian *Madonna* four years ago. She goes to Milan to see this picture she is working on, then skips a committee meeting to go to Padua. Here she delivers a letter to a man who also sold a Titian two years ago. Finally, preoccupied and excited, she begins to rewrite her paper about her discoveries, and is murdered before she can deliver it.

"She uncovered an unofficial element of the committee's work that had developed in recent years. In all three cases, Roberts, the stylistic expert, made the visual assessment and Kollmar, the archive man, dealt with the documentary evidence and wrote the reports. Two of the pictures were sold and Roberts tried to make money out of all of the operations.

"The first two were simple. The speed of operation of the Titian committee was not great under the old regime. Kollmar's beavering away in the archives and checking of facts could take up to eighteen months. Very frustrating for an owner who wants to sell and needs a reputable authentication to get the maximum price.

"In the first case it appears that it wasn't even Roberts' idea. It was the owner in St Gall who suggested that Roberts receive a five per cent cut of the sale price in exchange for his personal authentication. The deal works very nicely, and Roberts gets a fat cheque for one hundred and twenty thousand dollars—none of which, incidentally, gets passed on to Dr Kollmar. The second time round he takes the initiative and suggests the arrangement himself.

"Why not? The pictures are probably genuine and Roberts knows he will be able to pressure Kollmar into the appropriate recommendation if there is any trouble. On the other hand, it is not entirely ethical, and if it became public that the great Anthony Roberts was enriching himself by selling his services in such a way it would probably compromise the Titian committee's integrity beyond easy repair.

"Also, of course, it would damage Roberts' reputation and it was the need to defend his honour that led to this unfortunate chain of events. Exposure as a man whose willingness to recognise Titians depended on how much money he got in return would be devastating. Even some-

one like Dr Kollmar might turn against him and he would
then be easy meat for Lorenzo.

"Everything goes very nicely indeed until the Milan
picture comes up for investigation. Benedetti wants to
sell and Roberts is tempted to repeat the operation even
though he doesn't need the money and the profit will be
fairly small. But, under Dr Lorenzo's new regime, the
work pace has speeded up and Kollmar is having to produce his reports more rapidly. The time span between
seeing the picture and a final decision is now too short,
especially as a lot of the necessary evidence in this case
has already been unearthed by Georges Bralle.

"So Roberts, quite simply, suppresses Bralle's evidence and hints to Kollmar that the picture is not worth
much. Kollmar recommends rejection. Roberts then of-
fers a personal authentication on the usual terms, intend-
ing to produce the suppressed evidence after the sale has
gone ahead and get the committee to reverse its decision.

"Very simple, but a mistake. Roberts goes beyond the
bounds of even the most liberal notion of ethics and gets
found out. The crucial fact was that Benedetti consulted
Bralle, who works out what is going on and is outraged.
That is why he says Kollmar hasn't made a mistake. He
thinks that Kollmar is part of the scheme. He starts
searching to see whether this has happened before."

A loud protest here from Kollmar, puce in the face
because of what he had heard. "That is outrageous. The
idea that someone of Roberts' position would act so
shamelessly—"

Bottando was about to interrupt, but the job was taken
out of his hands. "Oh shut up, you pompous old fool,"
Kollmar's wife said. She spoke in German, but the general import was tolerably clear. "There's no need to
prove you're a simpleton, is there?"

Bottando smiled at her. "Thank you, madam," he said. "You see, the point to note is that Roberts told Signorina di Stefano that he had no opinion about the painting's merits, but told Kollmar he thought it was worthless. Why contradict himself? There can be no reason at all unless he wanted to distance himself from that opinion, and place all the responsibility for the decision on Dr Kollmar."

Having patiently explained to the German that his defence of his erstwhile colleague was perhaps unwise, Bottando decided that it was time to get back to his argument before he forgot what it was.

"Now, Roberts is worried when Masterson decides to examine the picture herself and wonders what she is up to. Efforts to deflect her come to nothing and he gets worried. As he never really took her abilities seriously, he naturally suspects she has also seen Bralle's evidence and may use it against him. He has to know what is going on, and so visits Bralle to find out.

"We know this because Bralle's diary says so. As Van Heteren told us, Bralle was much given to slightly malicious nicknames. Dr Van Heteren, what did he call Roberts?"

Van Heteren stirred himself out of the moody reverie that suggested strongly he was only half listening to what was going on, and blinked at Bottando.

"Well," he said hesitantly, "because of his pious demeanour and stately appearance, he always used to refer to him as St Anthony."

Bottando smiled happily at him. "And in Bralle's diary, it says that St Anthony was going to visit on the day of the murder.

"On top of that, he said Masterson was to write a reference for Miller. Of the people in Venice, only Masterson and Van Heteren knew this. Masterson did not want it spread around. So how did Roberts know? Simply that a copy of Bralle's letter recommending her was on his desk in Balazuc. Where Roberts had seen it.

"What transpired at the meeting in Balazuc is impossible to know, of course. But it seems likely that Bralle accused Roberts of unprofessional behaviour and threatened to expose him in order to save his committee. He was murdered in a way which made it look as though old age had caught up with him. It was the only possible way of keeping him quiet. Roberts no doubt reckoned the old man would die soon anyway."

A great communal sigh followed this announcement. So it was Roberts. As the blame for everything was swung carefully on to a dead man, the atmosphere in the room lightened noticeably. Only Van Heteren still seemed aware of the tragic dimensions of the past few day's events.

"When Roberts got back to Venice, he was probably fairly confident that all would be well," Bottando continued. "Bralle was out of the picture and there was no evidence Masterson had been in contact with him. But then he borrowed her book and found a ticket to St Gall. He knew she was working on the Milan picture, and then he hears she has gone to Padua. Finally, Van Heteren says she is rewriting her paper and reckons it will be a sensation. He knows what sort of sensation, and that it will have nothing to do with an analysis of brush-strokes in the early work of Titian.

"Of course, Roberts had an impeccable alibi for Masterson's murder. He made sure of that, by buying opera tickets at the last minute. And he could not have stolen the Marchesa's pictures."

There was a scuffle at the back of the room, as Bovolo

and another policeman sidled in, the former with quiet triumph on his face. Bottando noticed and grew alarmed. A man like that didn't look happy without a good reason.

"It is often said that one murder leads to another," he resumed, hoping that things were not about to go badly wrong. "This is not the case here, as Roberts was much too careful to chance his luck a second time around."

It was a statement which caused some upset. Having narrowed the field down in a satisfactory way for those present, he was now opening it up again.

"There have been a lot of pictures in this case, Titians in Milan and Padua, other works stolen from the Marchesa. Odd parallels kept on surfacing. One Titian is of a woman being stabbed in a garden; Masterson was stabbed in a garden. The murderer in the picture was a jealous husband and Masterson's lover, Van Heteren, by his own admission, was jealous. It was almost as if history was repeating itself and pointing at the culprit.

"But all this was mere diversion, as we eventually realised. Van Heteren's jealousy was aroused by mischievous comments by Dr Miller, the only other person who urgently wanted Masterson out of the way. Is that not true, doctor?"

He didn't want to comment, it seemed. He took over from Van Heteren in the study of the floor, white-faced and silent. All he managed was a shake of the head.

"Let me say what happened, then. At lunch on Friday, Miller and Roberts ate together. It is clear how Roberts laid out his case. He dropped his bombshell that Masterson was writing Miller's reference, and added for good measure that she would probably go all out to get him thrown out of his job. Miller could well believe it, considering the remarks she had made the day before. On top of that, Roberts told him that the paper she would deliver on the following Monday would seal his fate. Although it was a tissue of lies, it would temporarily at least damage the status of the committee and wreck Roberts' reputation and ability to act on Miller's behalf.''

Bottando noticed that Flavia was looking slightly unhappy here, and became worried he was running off the tracks. So he paused to take a sip of water and leant over to her. ''Am I going wrong?'' he whispered urgently.

She waggled her hand from side to side. ''Go ahead. I'll tell you later.''

He put the glass down and tried to remember where he was. ''As was obvious to Signorina di Stefano, Miller had a deep resentment of Masterson. She had better contacts, produced books, had a better job. Now she was going to destroy him. Is it surprising that, when Roberts said she had to be stopped, he agreed fervently?

''But Miller had a perfect alibi. He was on the island at ten, when he was seen in the kitchen, and no boats landed at the island throughout the evening. Consequently, he must have been there earlier and could not have killed Masterson in the Giardinetti Reali.

''Except for the fact that he had no need of a boat. He overheard Kollmar offer Masterson a drink. That offer took place on the boat leaving the island. So he did leave; that is clear. How did he get back if no boats were running? He must have managed it somehow.

''This is what happened. Earlier in the day, Roberts had taken a message for Masterson and so he knew where to find her. This information he mentioned to Miller over lunch. Miller then takes the boat over and wanders around, working himself up into an even greater rage. He goes to the garden to find her and argue with her. He accuses her of wanting to destroy him, of viciousness and malice. Roberts says this, Roberts tells me that. She probably tells him, as she had the day before, that he is being ridiculous and making a mountain out of a molehill. He snaps. He stabs her with a penknife and leaves her for dead.

"Was this premeditated or not? I don't know. Perhaps he only meant to give her a piece of his mind. But the insinuations of Roberts, combined with years of deep-seated jealousy sent him over the edge. She had it coming. Her own fault.

"But he has a problem. The idea of giving himself up doesn't appeal, and he is stuck far from his room with no way of getting back. But it's only about five hundred metres across the canal, a few lengths of a swimming pool. Nothing that could not be handled by someone who is such a powerful and practised swimmer. He kicks off his shoes, then drops them, the knife and her bag in the canal.

"When he reaches the Isola San Giorgio he lets himself in a side door with his key. He is soaking, and so leaves puddles of water in the corridor which are mistaken for a leaky roof. It was not raining. How else did they get there? He dries himself, goes down to the laundry room to wash out his clothes, then asks for a glass of water to establish an alibi. Any comments yet, doctor?"

No reply, yet again.

"But Masterson wasn't dead," he went on. "She knows she is dying and won't get help in time. She also knows from Miller that he was put up to it by Roberts, playing Iago to Miller's Othello. Appropriate Venetian metaphor, I think. She tries to leave some hint of what has happened.

"She isn't dragged to the greenhouse, as Commissario Bovolo thought. She crawls there herself, because she

knows what's inside. It contains flowers she had specifically chosen herself to decorate the table at Saturday's
banquet. She tears the crucifix off her neck and grasps a
flower. A cross and a lily. The symbol of St Anthony.
The flowers were meant to be a triumphant reference to
her discovery in Milan, but turned into her wreath.''

A lengthy pause as everybody swivelled to look hard
at the silent, white-faced Miller. ''Well, Dr Miller. How
close are we?'' Bottando asked eventually.

''Close,'' he said with the weariness of a man who has
had enough. ''Very close.''

''Do you want to make a formal statement? They work
wonders for the sentence and help get a reduced charge.
Alternatively, you can wait until we find some trace of
blood on your clothes or under your fingernails. We will
find something. These forensic people always do. They're
awfully good, you know.''

In fact, he was doubtful about the scientific investigation. This forensic business was never as good as the
experts claimed. He'd seen too many authenticate fake
paintings to have all that much faith in their prowess, but
it seemed to convince Miller, who nodded in miserable
agreement. Bottando sighed with relief.

''Good,'' he said with satisfaction as he noticed the
increasingly jaundiced appearance of Bovolo's face. He
was a man seeing his promotion vanish before his very
eyes.

''Hold on a second, are you telling me that Dr Miller
here also killed Roberts?'' This was Kollmar, calmer now
and beginning to take an active interest in the proceedings. Bottando wished he wasn't. He felt uncomfortable
about the next stage. But Flavia insisted it was tactically
necessary. Before he could start talking, she took over.
He had a feeling she didn't trust him somehow.

"No, of course he didn't," she said briskly. "Why should he? The sequence of events is quite clear. Roberts is questioned. He tells his story; how he is upset about Masterson's death, how he tried to do so much for her, and so on. And does a very good job. No suspicion attaches to him at all.

"But later on I also see Van Heteren," who began to turn pale once more at the statement, "and mention the lily and crucifix motif. Because of my somewhat impressionistic method of questioning, he is the only person I told.

"Dr Van Heteren is no fool. He realises that Masterson was indicating Roberts, but can't believe it. Nor does he want to incriminate a colleague falsely, which was why he refused to tell us he had overheard Roberts talking to Pianta on the phone.

"So on Tuesday evening, after I have seen him, he goes over to discuss the matter. Roberts reassures him, but knows that although the carabinieri are unlikely to realise what the symbols mean, there is a chance that we will. And if this leads to Bralle's death being investigated more closely . . ."

No harm in a bit of publicity, she thought. Especially in a good cause. "Roberts is trapped and cannot face the idea of jail and humiliation. He has already murdered and manipulated to avoid it, but it is clear that the effort has not been worthwhile. There is no way out, so after Van Heteren has left he kills himself to avoid the inevitable. He tries hanging first, hence the red marks around his neck, but hasn't enough courage to go through with it. So he jumps in the canal and drowns."

Bottando looked even more uncomfortable, Argyll was wearing an expression of considerable surprise, and the rest of the audience breathed another huge sigh of relief.

"That's the way it was, was it not, doctor?" she asked the Dutchman.

Van Heteren did not reply for some time. Then he glanced up from the carpet, which he had been studying with enormous interest and said quietly, "If you say so."

"And you did overhear that phone conversation?"

"Yes," he said. "But—"

"Good," said Flavia, interrupting him. "Pity you didn't tell us earlier, but I knew it was something along those lines."

She smiled reassuringly at her boss, who frowned back. At least the worst was over. He shifted in his seat and decided to get this miserable business over as quickly as possible. Complete triumph was only a matter of minutes away. He merely wished he knew what little surprise Bovolo had in store for them.

"Now, then," he said, taking control once more. "One last mystery. The Marchesa's pictures. These had an ambiguous status. The Marchesa's husband did what many aristocrats do. His estate went to his heir, Dr Lorenzo, with his wife having rights to it for as long as she lived. Nothing could be sold without Lorenzo's permission. Which, of course, he gave for these works, because they were of no importance.

"But the Marchesa and Signora Pianta had a suspicion that this was not the case with one picture, an anonymous portrait. Louise Masterson was keen to examine it, but would not say why. If it was valuable, and if Dr Lorenzo found out, he would undoubtedly withdraw his agreement, because of his public role as defender of the National Heritage.

"The Marchesa loathed the idea of having to do as she was told by someone so much younger—a perfectly understandable trait, I must say. I have recently suffered similar difficulties myself. Signora Pianta was thinking of her old age, and the fact that she might well be homeless and penniless once her employer died. Again perfectly understandable.

"Once Masterson died and there was a possibility her interest in the work would emerge, it became clear that the picture would have to be got out of the country quickly, before Lorenzo vetoed the idea. They were, of course, determined not to draw attention to themselves, which is why Signora Pianta failed to explain the appointment with Masterson just before she was murdered.

"So at the last minute they started trying to renegotiate the deal with Argyll, to pressure him to smuggle it to Switzerland. Unfortunately for them he refused and they fell back on an alternative little plot. It is not surprising Signora Pianta was so upset when Argyll introduced her to my assistant that evening, consider what they were about to do.

"Quite simply, they moved the pictures down to a rarely used cellar and reported them stolen to gain time in which to find a more corrupt dealer. The picture could then be smuggled out, sold through an intermediary and Lorenzo could do little about it. So, when I realised what must have happened, I had a policeman stationed there to stop it leaving the house."

Pianta was white-faced with horror, the Marchesa had the air of a cheeky adolescent caught stealing biscuits. She looked, in fact, rather pleased. She, at least, had thoroughly enjoyed herself in the past few days.

"Very well done indeed, General," she said, beaming with delight. "And I take it back entirely. Not *all* policemen are stupid."

Bottando inclined his head to accept the compliment.

"My dear auntie, *really*," Lorenzo said severely.

"How could you? There is no question of Pianta being thrown on to the streets and you know it. I always knew you were wayward, I never thought you were that bad." She shrugged naughtily, looking at him with twinkling eyes.

"But what about my pictures?" Argyll interjected, trying to get some basic information about the really important question.

"Of course, there is no question now . . ." Lorenzo began, but was interrupted by a quiet cough from the back of the room. A discreet cough. Almost modest, for Commissario Bovolo. Argyll thought it a strangely ominous noise.

"Before you go on," he said, with just a hint of satisfaction in his voice.

There was a brief pause as the Venetian enjoyed the rarity of being the focal point of the evening. "Go on, then," Bottando suggested gloomily. Here it comes, he thought.

"In accordance with General Bottando's suggestions," he said somewhat stiffly, "when it was ascertained that the Marchesa and Signora Pianta had left the building, we entered with a warrant and searched in the cellars for the missing items. It was not easy, which is why we were late. As you know, the weather has been bad and the tides heavy . . ."

He was interrupted by a strangled sound coming from Lorenzo. The Marchesa's eyes lost their twinkle and Argyll, although he had no idea what was coming, decided he didn't want to hear it. Bovolo, however, proceeded inexorably on his way.

"The cellar is one of those which communicates directly with the canal outside, to facilitate easy access to the building for tradesmen. It would appear that most of the paintings were placed directly on the floor, propped up to keep them from damage, but not sufficiently elevated . . ."

"Oh, Pianta, you fool. Can't you do anything properly?" the Marchesa broke in.

"Not sufficiently elevated, as I say," resumed Bovolo sententiously, "to stop them being dislodged by the high tides which at some stage today began to flood the room. Several of the pictures were discovered by my officers still in the cellar, floating on the surface of the water. They have suffered badly, but they have been recovered."

"And the portrait?" asked Argyll weakly. Stoicism in such circumstances is all a human being has left.

"The portrait in question," resumed Bovolo, now on the last lap, "which I was particularly requested by General Bottando to recover, appears to be one of those washed out by the tidal movements into the lagoon. We will, of course, search for it tomorrow morning . . ."

"Oh, Jesus, don't bother," said Lorenzo, with a light and nervous laugh. "After twelve hours in salt water there won't be anything left to find. The only consolation we have is the hope that it was not really valuable after all."

Argyll looked at them all, noticing that most were far more upset about the loss of the picture than they were about the murder of Masterson or Bralle. Pathetic, really. He also saw Flavia glaring at him in what appeared to be blind panic. It was too much to say that her eyes were popping out of her head with alarm, but clearly she wanted to tell him something.

He closed his mouth, then opened it again. Then hesitated. This was not at all how he had imagined his evening ending. What about his triumph? His great coup? Ah, the things you do for friends.

"Well, what about it?" Lorenzo prodded, when he decided he could stand watching Argyll's mouth flap about no more. "Was it valuable?"

Argyll rubbed his face wearily in his hands, sniffed loudly and gazed around the room at the ranks of expectant faces hoping he wasn't going to say anything too distressing.

"I stand by my original assessment, for what it's worth. I've been through all the evidence carefully. A minor work by a minor artist. Nothing that would set the sale rooms alight, of that I can assure you," he concluded.

Everybody but himself and Commissario Bovolo seemed more than content with this explanation. Grateful, even. He stood up morosely and, as there seemed nothing else to say, everybody else began to stand as well. Bit by bit, the meeting broke up. Little fragments of desultory conversation broke out as people got their coats and prepared to depart.

Miller was being watched by Bovolo's assistant before being taken to make his statement. His colleagues studiously ignored him. Bottando and the magistrate were deep in a conversation from which Bovolo was ostentatiously excluded. Lorenzo eyed his aunt as though assessing the wisdom of approaching her, then evidently decided to let her stew. Kollmar and his wife walked quietly out, followed by a still beaming Marchesa with Pianta bringing up the rear.

Eventually only Van Heteren was left. He came quietly up to Flavia and opened his mouth to speak.

"No. I don't want to hear any more, doctor," she said

briskly before he could even begin. "Go away. Go back to Holland."

"But I must—"

"You must nothing of the sort. I have had more than enough. Go home and go to bed. Now."

"Ever thought of taking up motherhood?" Argyll asked as he watched the abashed and chastened Dutchman scuttle out of the room to obey her command. "You did that like a natural."

"No," she replied. "But thank you for the offer. Come on. Let's get out of here."

The rain, at least, had cleared the atmosphere. The damp, humid oppressiveness had gone, and in its place was a light, fresh breeze and crystal clear night. Even the flood tide had gone down a little. Another hour or so and the streets would be clear.

In total, and not very happy, silence, the two Italians and the Englishman were ferried back across the wide opening of the Grand Canal.

"That was a fine piece of work," Bottando said eventually, patting her lightly on the shoulder. "My congratulations. I'm proud of you. You may well keep your job."

"Thank you," she replied. "I'm not sure about some of the details, though."

"Nor am I," cut in Argyll. "I mean, when you said . . ."

Flavia placed her hand on his arm and gave it a slight warning squeeze to make him shut up. He lapsed into a resentful silence.

"I noticed you were unhappy. Did I go wrong somewhere?" asked Bottando.

"You got the right man," she said, "but I think you

missed the point about her death. That's because you didn't understand her.''

"Oh, yes? What's wrong with my understanding?''

"All you lot characterised her in a way which was, if I may say so, perfectly predictable. Pushy, aggressive, ambitious, vindictive. You assumed, like them, that she was going to dig her fangs in.''

"And you're going to tell me she wasn't?''

"Of course she wasn't. It doesn't fit. It is what Roberts thought, and that's why he put Miller up to it. But he was wrong. I don't think she gave a hoot about what he was up to, beyond disapproving and wanting to quit the committee before Bralle let rip. She went to St Gall because she wanted to hear about Benedetti's Titian from Bralle. She went to Milan and Padua for the same reason. She didn't even meet either of the men who had sold those pictures.

"Masterson didn't want to get involved. Why should she, when Bralle was already plotting to expose Roberts? We know she had no time for that sort of thing. She was irritated about Kollmar, no doubt, but it was only Roberts who said she'd been offensive about him. No one else heard her be anything but polite. In the committee meeting last year she merely said she wanted to work on the picture; it was Roberts who told Kollmar she was being nasty about him behind his back. OK, she was brusque, but who wouldn't be with that pedantic little ninny?

"With Van Heteren, Benedetti or that friar in Padua, she was charming and kind. They all said so. And on her last day she wasn't in the library writing denunciations about academic corruption or bad references for Miller, she was reading art history. Like the good, dedicated scholar she was. She was never any sort of danger to Roberts or Miller. The poor woman was murdered simply because they all thought she was just as self-obsessed, mean and ambitious as they were themselves.''

"So what was this paper going to be about?"

"She was going to announce one of the most sensational finds for years," she said simply. "That was what she was working on so hard. Not politics and denunciations."

Bottando winced and held up his hand. "Stop there. I don't want to know. You may be right, and perhaps I did the poor lady an injustice, but I can't stand to hear the details. Besides, I do seem to have arrested the right man and all I care about now, frankly, is drying my feet off and getting on the next plane back to Rome," he said as the boat nudged against the landing stage and he levered himself heavily out.

"I have a budget submission and a large amount of last-minute lobbying to do first thing tomorrow morning. Still," he said more cheerfully, "at least there is some ammunition to do it with now."

So she dropped it. Bottando had set his heart on a hot bath and hurried off the moment the boat touched the quay. Argyll and she strolled off on their own, and within ten minutes had got themselves totally lost once more.

"Now you can ask your question," she said after Bottando had disappeared and they'd given up trying to decide where they were.

"Ah. Which one is that?"

"The one about Van Heteren."

"Oh, that. Well, yes. He did it, didn't he?"

"Of course he did. He went over to see Roberts, accused him of murdering his lover, half-throttled him, dragged him to the canal and threw him in. Those marks under Roberts' house—and on his neck—prove that.

Crime of Passion. Impetuous man, just the sort of thing he would do. Told you he was like that.''

"But it was the wrong man. Roberts hadn't killed Masterson. You didn't feel like mentioning that? And Bottando agreed?"

She shrugged. "Not our murder investigation. It wouldn't have done to have humiliated the locals totally. As it is, this splits Bovolo and the magistrate apart. Bovolo is ground in the dust a bit for being wrong about Masterson, the magistrate is so happy no one mentioned the way he leant on the pathologist that he has agreed to thank us in writing for our excellent work. And Pierre Janet, dear sweet man, will also say what heroes we are for solving Bralle's murder. The department covered in glory just in time for Bottando's budget submissions. What more could anybody want?"

"Oh, come on," he said with exasperation. "Neither you nor Bottando are that cynical. Are you?"

"No," she admitted. "But I couldn't bring myself to do it. Nor could the General, once I'd worked on him a bit. He took a bit of persuading, but he's an old softie really and quite open to reason as long as no one knows about it."

"Hmph. I still think you're being a little over-generous. He is a murderer, after all."

"True, and I'm sure he feels rotten about it. But Roberts was responsible for it all and did kill Bralle. A nasty man in every way. And dead, too. Nothing we could do could bring him back. Van Heteren, on the other hand, was the only likeable person amongst them. He really loved that woman and was the only person who ever gave her a chance.

"I find it all quite understandable, myself. Besides, what good would arresting him do? I've never really understood the idea that killers *have* to be delivered up to justice. Seems to me that some people deserve to get away with murder. Depending on who the victim is, of course. Wrong sort of reasoning for a policewoman, isn't it?''

"Sort of. But, as you keep on reminding me, you're not a policewoman, so I suppose you can reason however you like.''

"Apart from that, of course, Van Heteren did us a favour. I doubt that we could ever have arrested Roberts. We know he killed Bralle, but there is no proof that would stand up in a court. We couldn't have got him for manipulating Miller, and his picture dealing, however unethical, was not illegal. He would have got off unscathed but for Van Heteren. Doesn't really excuse Van Heteren, I suppose, if you want to be technical about it. But there you are.''

"So you cover it all up?''

"Us? Cover up a murder? Good heavens no. What an idea,'' she said smugly. "That's the beauty of it. We merely stated an opinion. There's nothing corrupt about being a bit askew over some details. As Bovolo kept on telling us, it was his case, nothing to do with us. He will have to withdraw his original report and write a new one, poor man. Very public and embarrassing for him. Of course, he will write it all down exactly as we described. He will describe the murder of Masterson and will go on to give the official opinion that Roberts committed suicide. Nifty, eh? It's not as if we're stopping him finding out the truth, if that's what he wants to do.''

Argyll went all quiet for a few moments and Flavia assumed he was lost in admiration. He wasn't, exactly; he was more trying to work out the moral implications of what she had just done. The effort defeated him, so he decided to give her the benefit of the doubt. There are some things foreigners in Italy can never really understand.

"The only difficulty was the Marchesa's picture," she said, wrapping her arm round him as a token of gratitude. "And fortunately you saved us from a nasty accident there. It would have been very awkward if you'd announced that Bottando's causing a policeman to be stationed in her house had indirectly resulted in the only Giorgione self-portrait in existence to be washed out to sea."

He looked at her with a puzzled expression on his face. "Giorgione?" he asked curiously. "What are you talking about? Who ever said anything about a Giorgione?"

She removed her arm. "You did," she began doubtfully.

"No, I didn't."

"Yes, you did. You said the picture was a self-portrait of Violante di Modena's lover . . ."

He burst out laughing. "Oh, no," he said in great delight. "I don't believe it. That's not what I meant at all. You poor thing. You must have been feeling dreadful for the past hour."

"What the hell did you mean then," she said crossly, annoyed she might have used so much sympathy and concern unnecessarily.

He cackled again. "I thought I'd told you. That picture of the man with the beaky nose was a self-portrait of a painter. The Padua series Titian *wanted* to paint showed this man a) accusing Violante di Modena of being unfaithful; b) murdering her; c) being poisoned himself. A bit odd, hijacking a religious commission for such things, but Titian was a young man and under great stress at the time. Maybe it was a sort of creative therapy. Not important, anyway.

"Obviously nothing to do with Giorgione, who died before Violante did and therefore can't have killed her. Besides, Giorgione died of a broken heart. I told you that. No one as famous as him could be murdered without somebody knowing. And on top of that, the portrait was as I described it, second-rate. Giorgione could paint better than that in his sleep.

"That wasn't what Masterson was getting at. She didn't think she'd found some lost masterpiece. It was the fact that she'd deciphered an intricate and personal account of a long-hidden scandal that excited her. Iconography, symbolism, reading pictures—that was her speciality, not painting style or archives. What not-very-nice man, to use her words, stole the lady and sent Giorgione to an early grave with a broken heart? And, it seems, killed her in a jealous fit when he thought she was falling in love with Titian? And then was poisoned himself in revenge for what he had done?

"The friar I talked to in Padua said the paintings were Titian's revenge, but he didn't realise what they were really about. Masterson cracked the account by putting all the bits together, reconstructing the Padua series and linking it with the Marchesa's portrait. Jolly clever of her, too."

"Come along, think," he said when she continued to look at him silently. "Titian would not have run off to Padua unless he'd done something daft. Violante's brother wouldn't have quashed proceedings against him if Titian hadn't restored family honour. And Pietro Luzzi did vanish, with a ridiculous story invented about his death in battle.

" 'The man died, and he disappeared.' That's St Anthony's inscription, but it also told the literal truth about Luzzi. Can you imagine the impact of an article, backed by an intricate, almost personal confession, proving that Titian poisoned Pietro Luzzi because he had stabbed one friend and caused another to die of grief?''

"Ah, I *see*," she said eventually with a huge sigh. "That is a relief. So all we have lost is a self-portrait by Pietro Luzzi?"

"Bravo. The grand finale, of course, came when Louise Masterson saw the link," he went on. "When Kollmar gave his verdict over that picture in Milan, she said nothing. But the same evening, she went to Lorenzo's party. She saw the portrait and that nose rang a bell, if noses can do that. She doesn't know what it means, but she starts thinking hard. An interesting face, she tells Van Heteren, but not a nice one. One that needs to be examined. There must be some sort of connection between it and the picture of Kollmar's they'd been talking about that morning, and she decides she is going to find out what it is. It is only after this that she announces she is going to work on Benedetti's picture herself.

"She needs to work fast when she hears the Marchesa's picture is up for sale, and even faster when Bralle tells her Benedetti's might go to the sale room as well. Someone else could also make the connection. So she starts running around. Milan, Padua, libraries in Venice. She begins frantically to rewrite the paper to add in the last bits of evidence she needs. Much to Van Heteren's irritation, of course. Roberts, I suppose, can't imagine anyone getting that excited over a mere picture. So when he tracks her movements he leaps fatally to the wrong conclusion. The rest you know.

"Violante was stabbed by Pietro Luzzi because of jealousy, Titian killed the murderer and the powers that be covered it up. Miller stabs Masterson because of a different sort of jealousy, Van Heteren takes his slightly inaccurate revenge, and the powers that be cover it up once more. Nice parallel, don't you think? History does repeat itself, it seems."

"And you expect me, and the rest of the world, to believe that?"

He shrugged once more. "Please yourself. But it's the only explanation I can think of for why he chose such a strange way of painting those murals in Padua. Not that it matters. I, certainly, am not going to give it much publicity."

"Why not?"

"I don't like being laughed at, basically. If I could prove it, that would be one thing. But proof depends on a proper examination of the Marchesa's portrait. Which, thanks to you, can't be done any more. It's gone forever. There aren't even any photographs; that agency didn't have any. I was waiting until I took delivery. Masterson was going to take some, but Miller got to her first. And, of course, without that, the story falls to bits and becomes nothing more than supposition, guesswork and fantasy.

"So," he concluded, "like Van Heteren, Titian will have to be left in peace, his reputation unsullied. Pity. I wouldn't have minded having the picture, but I suppose settling for Benedetti's Titian is a fair swap."

He looked to see how she was taking what he considered to be a masterly exposition.

"Well, I don't know," she said, thrusting her hands into her pockets in a gesture of discomfort. "Are you sure you're not just having a little joke at my expense?"

He gave her a whimsical glance which she considered decidedly ambiguous. "What's that?" he asked eventually.

Flavia was examining an envelope she'd found in her pocket and pulled out.

"The snaps I took of the landing stage under Roberts' house. The only real evidence against Van Heteren."

He took them and studied them by the light of a lamp-post. Then grinned at her, tore them in half and tossed them, piece by piece, into the canal, followed by the negatives. They watched them drift slowly off until they sank.

"If you're going to pervert the course of justice, do it properly, that's what I always say. Damn lagoon is awash with evidence tonight, it seems," he said. He put his arm round her, thinking such a gesture might be excusable in the circumstances.

"Ah, well. That tidies up the loose ends. Come on," he said, giving her a squeeze which, to his infinite pleasure, she returned. "I shall accompany you all the way back to your hotel room."

He steered her round until she was pointing in entirely the wrong direction. "This way, I think."